S0-BCL-880

Geraldine

Geraldine

David Watmough

Ekstasis Editions

a riverrun book

Library and Archives Canada Cataloguing in Publication

Watmough, David, 1926-
    Geraldine / David Watmough.

ISBN 978-1-894800-99-0

    I. Title.

PS8595.A8G47 2007   C813'.54   C2007-902306-1

© David Watmough 2007
Cover design: Miles Lowry
Author photograph: Floyd St.Clare

Published in 2007 by:
Ekstasis Editions Canada Ltd.   Ekstasis Editions
Box 8474, Main Postal Outlet   Box 571
Victoria, B.C. V8W 3S1   Banff, Alberta ToL oCo

THE CANADA COUNCIL | LE CONSEIL DES ARTS
FOR THE ARTS | DU CANADA
SINCE 1957 | DEPUIS 1957

BRITISH
COLUMBIA
ARTS COUNCIL
Supported by the Province of British Columbia

Geraldine has been published with the assistance of grants from
the Canada Council for the Arts and the British Columbia Arts
Council administered by the Cultural Services Branch of British
Columbia.

for Floyd St. Clair, without whom this book
would never have seen birth
and for Rick Archbold, without whom
it could not have been completed

also special thanks to Dr. Julia Levy
for her much-needed scientific expertise
and to Mac Elrod for his critical attention
and warmth of support over many years.

Chapter One

A Scrap of Paper

If I don't want any of them to see this, why the hell do I write it? I suppose it's a compulsion. I'm telling myself that I need to leave proof that I am not mad. Not some lonely old biddy who's gone crazy. That the old woman, way up there in her fancy apartment, who might take a swig or two more than is good for her and then tells all those assholes in Mayfair Lodge that she's sick to god-damn death of their patronizing, hasn't—repeat *hasn't*—lost her marbles.

Must make sure I print this out and then wipe it off the goddamn computer. Then tear up the paper. Or at least hide it so that none of my idiot family, or prying neighbors, — anyone else for that matter - gets a chance of seeing it before I'm stiff and cold and safe from the whole bloody lot of them.

Mind you—"you?" Who the hell are *you*? I'm talking about more than just the business yesterday that my solemn son will doubtless describe when he arrives in an hour or so as a "spree." I'm talking about *me* — yesterday, today, forever! I'm talking about the woman who dedicated sixty years—no, sixty-*five* by the time the bastards made me retire—of professional life to her fellow beings—fully aware that *that* easy title covers the bright and the idiotic, the old and the evil, the young and the forgiving, and not forgetting the huge majority who were drones and the tiny minority who were ambitious.

Of course, I'm talking about more than all that public stuff as I peck away at these characters on—what do they call it nowadays?—a keyboard?—because I am also angry. Very angry. Some years ago a colleague in Ottawa—we were there to raise funds for some research project, the ethical implications over genetic engineering it must've been (I bet it was that dumbbell, Carstairs, from Carleton) suddenly shouted out in the amphitheatre where we were sitting, "Dr. Butterfield, why are you so angry? We're here to get the government to do something positive for all of us across the country and all you can do is bitch and complain."

"I am angry," I told him, "And I will remain perpetually angry, because although there are flags for every province and territory on the walls of this room, there are only two that really count: the Feds' and Ontario's. And the province I represent under our rather silly, not to say vulgar, flag of British Columbia is the least relevant of all. I haven't been asked to say a single word, yet my colleagues and I at UBC—University of British Columbia—with my Unit in our Science Faculty have contributed major breakthroughs in genetic exploration and aired the ethical implications. *That*, sir, is why I'm angry."

Who knows? Perhaps back then that was the main reason. Though I could never tell if it was the shunning of British Columbia or my status as a mere woman. Then when wasn't it like that? When could I ever be certain whether it was my work or my gender being judged?

Not any more, of course. Not for all the years since I've been holed up in this apartment and seen those brown patches grow on the backs of both hands, watched the wrinkles deepen across buttocks, and veins grow blue on my withered calves. Not to mention the embarrassing drips and uncontrollable noises that mark my senescent state and drown what was once Professor Geraldine Butterfield, Member of the Royal Society, under the image of just an old woman who won't shut up, but who refuses to lie down and die.

And that's what I hate. Yet maybe, just maybe, in an odd way it's that which keeps me going. In any case, I've written enough. My wrists and fingertips ache. So now the distinguished holder of the Order of Canada is going back to the nursery where she will find the best, the most super hiding place for a print-out of this before I hit "erase"! Thank God I got 40 watt bulbs installed and the place is cluttered with junk. Anyone but me would break their neck searching for anything!

Chapter Two

Hugh's Turn

Anxious or annoyed neighbors called Mr. Molosovich, the apartment manager. He in turn called the old woman's son and that set the ball rolling. Dr. Hugh Butterfield, 58, General Physician, with a practice in White Rock, hard by the border between the U.S. and Canada, arrived in haste at his mother's eleventh-floor home, situated in Vancouver's tower-studded West End. Once more he envied her luxurious high-rise in Mayfair Lodge with its extravagant sweep of views. Its north side encompassed the soaring coastal mountains; the south and west aspects, which included his mother's own corner apartment, extended from volcanic-coned Mt. Baker visible from the extreme left of her curved balcony, past that of anchored freighters in the waters of English Bay, to the gray smudge of Vancouver Island which, on a clear day such as that April one, included the niveous tips of its central range.

He did not knock on her apartment door immediately. Visitors didn't arrive at the cream-painted doors along the carpeted corridors of Mayfair Lodge to announce themselves. For fear of startling, or even antagonizing his ninety-six-year-old mother by pressing her foyer button at the ground floor entrance, he had buzzed the supervisor, who had first spoken to him about her condition, and then let him into the quiet plush and soft light of the building.

Apart from his mother's variable attitude towards him depending wholly upon her mood that day, he had no wish to confront her without being first armed with some detailed knowledge of her condition from Molosovich. The manager-cum-janitor had 'phoned him and informed him in his struggling Serbian English with its total absence of definite articles that Dr. Geraldine Butterfield was wandering from floor to floor of his building, mumbling incomprehensibly and seemingly quite unaware of what year it was, let alone where she might be.

It seemed to the doctor that Anton Molosovich was implying that his oldest tenant had been drunk, but from painful experience her son knew he would need some concrete details of her condition before he sought corroborative proof in her apartment. He also wanted any other evidence from the voluble Serb that might help him decide on a course of action—including the names of those fellow tenants who had alerted the Manager of his mother's aberrant behavior in the first place. She was not disposed to take any charges of mis-behavior lightly—and that was particularly the case if it came from a filial source. On the two occasions he had attempted to persuade her to leave her home in the high-rise, he had been angrily shown the door.

Hugh made three distinct bangs with his knuckles after he thought he'd heard a movement in the hallway beyond. There was no knocker on the door, only the small hole that he had long ago discovered was designed to look out rather than in. For a moment, he stood there, hesitant: uncertain of his opening words when the door opened, uncertain for that matter, of what kind of condition he would find her in. Fearing, as always, the worst on *that* score, he thought his three knocks perhaps a little pretentious.

He recalled visits to Paris and plays at *The Comédie Française* which had always been heralded by the three loud bangs from the stage affirming the classical unities. Or was it the assertion of the Trinity of Father, Son, and Holy Ghost? He couldn't remember. All he knew was that it was a hell of a long time ago and that she had been with him in the French capital and that his much-needed holiday had not been a success.

But the floodgates of reverie were not to be opened. Her front door was instead. There she stood, cane in hand, screwing up her eyes and blinking as if it were darker than it really was—devoid, of course, of the spectacles he had given her and which she'd never worn in his presence.

"I knew it was you," she said, omitting his name and the fact he hadn't buzzed from below. "That silly *bang-bang-bang* you picked up in Paris when I got my honorary doctorate at The Sorbonne. Or was it the *Prix Curie,* it's slipped my memory."

"Can I come in, Mother?"

"Well you certainly can't spy on me out there very well, can you?"

"Mother!"

And that was the summary of their greeting, the first encounter between the venerable bio-chemist and her only son the spring of that year of 2002.

The sense of *déjà vu* as he followed in the wake of her unseasonably flimsy summer dress with its shoulder straps revealing her wrinkled, age-mottled flesh, was no comfort but rather profoundly oppressive. He wondered gloomily what he'd do with all the clutter that now surrounded them when she was gone. Not that he didn't want it. At least *some* of it.

There were several items he'd had his eye on for years and now that he was a widower he wouldn't have to do battle with pushy Eileen as he had over almost every stick of their furniture when decorating their own stucco home. As for the children, Jeremy and Rebecca were powerless when it came to his declared will and wants. They couldn't fall out with him as he had so often with his own mother, because they desperately wanted his money. And as bolster to that, his single-parent daughter had embraced some Born-Again crap and was told Sunday after Sunday to "honour her parents" and affect love for them.

"What brings you to my place this time, Hugh? That stupid janitor been yakking?"

"Apparently you disturbed half the building on your last rampage." Hugh espied a brown bottle of Ballantine's whisky—presumably emptied—in the otherwise vacant aquarium, which had known no replacements since she'd let the first contingent of tropical fish rise belly-up to the surface. "You been into that again?" He pointed with his thumb at the bottle.

"Regularly. At six o'clock when I serve cocktails. Am I to assume that you, my child, now that your wife has departed, live without any of the social graces? If so, Hugh, may I suggest that is a very imprudent thing to do? The person living alone is even more in need of social structures to maintain a balanced life and a proper perspective."

He was about to make his usual protest about her addressing him as if he were attending one of her famous lectures back in the fifties and sixties But he had the more agreeable task of correcting her over a matter of fact. "I'm not living alone. Jeremy has returned. Been back for months. The thing with Graham didn't work out. But that's not why I'm here instead of seeing my patients this morning."

Geraldine had reached her favorite armchair, facing, through the plate glass, a liberating expanse of water. Sitting down, she nodded her thinning head of white hair towards her son and the twin chair next to her. She waited until he was settled before she spoke again. But she stared out at her balcony rather than at the doctor. "I get depressed from time to time. Who doesn't? But if every time that happened to someone they were moved into an institution we'd soon run out of places to lock them up, wouldn't we?"

"A bout of depression hardly covers what I've been told, Mother." He forbore to add that most depressed weren't ninety-six. Nor did he deem it a right moment to bring up again the subject of her entering a retirement home. "I've always told you I can provide you with medication—especially as you seem unable to get on with any doctors here in Vancouver."

Geraldine smirked. "I think I hear professional jealousy, child. Anyway, Caskie has served me for the past year or so. He's a fool, of course, and treats me as if I hadn't forgotten more pharmaceutics than he's ever learned. But he provides me with bliss pills when I want, and that's all I ask."

"What happened yesterday, then, when you went a wandering? He run out of medication for you?"

"You have obviously been well primed by our gossipy Serb downstairs. And probably by that retired Bay saleswoman Mrs. Solway, and I expect by that idiot ex-insurance peddler that I bumped into on the second floor. He and his wife detest me because I've had occasion to complain about their vulgar music which blares upwards when I'm sitting outside on the balcony. He once asked me whether I'd been a lab assistant at UBC. I told him that I'd been rejected when I applied but got a job as groundskeeper instead. I think if I'd told him I was a member of the Royal Society he would have thought I was a domestic at Buckingham Palace or something!"

"Mother, does it ever occur to you that there are people who might think you're a snob?"

"Legitimate pride in one's career, child, is not to be confused with believing one is superior in all things—except, that is, over such oafs who live in this building and have no sense whatever of history—let alone of what I accomplished single-handed as a woman over sixty fighting years." She held her slightly wobbly head high.

He let that go. It was hardly the first time he'd heard such sentiments from her. But as she never seemed capable of providing him with any respect for what he'd succeeded in doing in building up a large and reasonably successful practice from scratch, why should he go spend time lauding her efforts? After all, he told himself for the umpteenth time, he'd paid for all her accomplishments as a world-renowned scientist in her field of bio chemistry by a lonely and unhappy childhood. Nor was it his fault that she'd succeeded in straggling through to this advanced age with its inevitable accumulation of physical aches and pains to which was now added the cost of falling out of scientific fashion and what she called *the attenuated memories of the masses.*

She wasn't through with him yet, though. "While you're here, Hugh, I'd like to put in an order for more of that ointment you came up with for my bed sores. And would you please slip across the Border again and get me more of that analgesic, Aleve. Why this stupid country wont allow naproxen sodium tablets of 220 mg's is beyond me!"

"You know the BCMA could take my license away if I was caught."

"Do you want me to take the Greyhound down to Blaine and get it myself?"

He felt too weary to reply. "Can I get you to promise me that if you have another of those *depression attacks,* you'll call me first? I'm warning you, Mother. One more time and that Molosovich or someone will get you carried out of this place, whether you want it or not."

She sat up as erectly as she could manage given her widow's peak, tapped her cane firmly by her stockinged foot. There was nothing like a threat to strengthen her resolve, in fact to send fresh energy coursing through her aging frame. "In which case, my son, it will be literally over my dead body. Once more I suggest you get it into your head that whether I'm considered just a piece of flotsam, whether there is anyone but you left to remember whom my work has benefited—for that matter, whether I am bloody well liked or whether I'm bloody well loathed—I shall stay here for as long as I bloody well wish! Is that clear?"

In spite of herself, her reedy voice was made more so by her trembling. (Although she had enjoyed the excuse to use "bloody" thrice.)

"Of course it's clear, Mother. In any case, I know damn well I'd be the last to be able to convince you otherwise. God Almighty! Poor old Dad persuaded me of that years ago!" (Hugh, too, had fallen into stronger language than was customary for him.)

"Well we won't invoke the dead, will we? Besides, there was a whole lot more that he didn't persuade you of—if he had, you'd be a happier man than you are today and a good deal more than a GP out there in the remote suburbs."

Hugh got up. "I'll send you the medications by express. You should have them tomorrow. Don't get up, I'll see myself out."

He no longer tried to kiss her on arrival or departure. She insisted the risk of disease transmission was too great at her age. (And, in any case, she was inclined to drool.)

He did, however, save a final round of ammunition to the very last moment. As his hand went up to the door handle he turned and called back. "Now do promise, Mother, to be civil if any of your fellow apartment owners come to visit. Try and remember that you are a little old lady whom they want to comfort."

He didn't wait for her response.

Chapter Three

Woman to Woman

Geraldine put down her phone and took a swig of her Ballantine's. She was not in a good mood. In spite of the sunny enticement of the day beyond the balcony, there was the more immediate fact that her diarrhea seemed to have increased over the twenty-four hours since her son's visit. She had just answered a call from her youngest grandchild, Rebecca, who hadn't deigned to visit her grandmother since her twenty-first birthday two years earlier, but thought she was compensating for her sloth by pestering her with phone calls that were as vacuous as they were inopportune, usually occurring when the old lady was making one of her all too frequent and debilitating trips to the bathroom.

The inconvenience of the poor timing was the least of it. There was the *content* of the calls. At the best of times, and with few exceptions, Geraldine did not favor today's young. She deplored their bulky garb, their self-indulgent habits, and, above all, their slovenly speech. Rebecca qualified as a brat on all these counts but earned further degrees of contempt by spattering her speech with references to the

Lord Jesus and the joyous space He was occupying in her life and could play in her grandmother's—if she would only open her heart and let Him in.

In vain had Geraldine told her that her quadruply by-passed heart still had its lifetime occupant and that she wasn't minded to share it with *any* man at her age. Nor, she had added, was her mind so untenanted that it could afford to waste time on superstitious nonsense and imbecilic beliefs that affronted the science she had faithfully served during her entire existence. On her better, more vigorous days, she also opined contempt for that phony comfort designed for those who couldn't abide their own company and were likewise afraid to confront bleak truth, such as the prospect of agonizing illness and the final fact of death.

Invariably her grandmother replied with some soppy remark about the need to agree to differ, followed by the insolent addition that she's a cub of a girl still fresh from her diapers (or at least her ugly dental braces), would persist in praying for her. Nevertheless, after such telephonic encounters, Geraldine was often left feeling drained from the sheer act of talking (rather as she had felt yesterday after her interview with stubborn Hugh) and uncomfortably aware that, the Jesus nonsense notwithstanding, there were days when her arthritis made her whimper and nights when she lay awake in her large double bed unable to achieve sleep yet soberly aware that, if she did, she might return to unsavory dreams or, even bleaker, that she might never wake up at all...

It was in that kind of mood, the specifics removed or somewhat sunk by a further draught of Scotch, that she returned to that little instrument that had paradoxically come to mean so much to her in these last years, and called Deborah Tregaskis in the suite immediately below her.

Once or twice, when her gnarled hands were trembling too much, she had forsaken the phone and banged with her perpetually dry mop on a space she estimated was right above Deborah's kitchen. But it was a practice she was determined to hold in check. It was, she reflected, so basic, so primitive, while she was still, regardless of the weight of all her years, the energetic champion of any technology reflecting *Homo sapiens'* ability to transcend physical space and effort. And Deborah Tregaskis, whom she was pleased to call her friend (though not telling everyone of the fact), was the last person she wished to appear before as other than the veteran woman biochemist who had smashed the white-coated patriarchy of the research labs and brought female scientists of every feather, eye to eye and nose to nose with the Cricks and Watsons of her era.

By the time she got the receiver precisely over her hearing aid she had her words fully prepared: "Debbie, dear. Could you possibly come up for—for a coffee or something. I'm suffering from a surfeit of family and desperately need an antidote!"

She flopped back with relief in her armchair when Deborah answered as usual in the affirmative. She looked about her. Noted the half emptied glass on her side table, the just-opened bottle on the never-played baby grand, the dead daffs she'd been meaning to get rid of for the past week, the lavatory door still open. But she did nothing. She didn't have to, she told herself with a smile. Not having to pretend that you still lived a neat and orderly life is what friends were for.

When there finally came the characteristically timid

tap at the door, she got slowly up and ambled unsteadily towards it. She felt no reason to hurry, Deborah being old enough to appreciate that at a certain stage in life, all movement became time-consuming. When she reached the door she was vaguely surprised to see that, after her son's departure, she had added the security chain to the lock. She smiled. She must have been subconsciously responding to the thought that she'd wished to see no more people that day, regardless of what challenges to body and mind the night would bring.

Now, however, she was eager for a fresh face—especially one not etched with disapproval. When she opened the door and confronted Deborah, the woman twenty years her junior, automatically bent her head down to kiss her. But Geraldine short-circuited her, quickly raising bloodless lips and pressing them on her friend's less shrunken and powdery cheek—thus reversing the usual choreography of greeting between them. Geraldine thought she could smell *eau de cologne*, but nowadays her sense of smell was highly erratic. She made no comment.

Deborah was wearing a pale-blue cashmere sweater over a grey skirt and simple brogues. On a red cord round her neck hung a pair of sunglasses. She fingered them. "I was sitting outside enjoying the morning when you called. Do you feel up to doing the same, Geraldine? Your balcony is so much grander than mine, what with that marvelous view of everything."

It had been far from the old lady's mind. Nevertheless she winked at her friend before giving her arm a tug. "Why not? As long as I'm not too far from you-know-where. That's why I leave the bathroom door open—in case I have to rush."

The retired Biology teacher smiled knowingly. She knew how Geraldine liked to speak freely with her of topics she'd have hated to share with anyone else. It gave Deborah a sense of being wanted—even while she knew her friend was inclined to patronize her for her having been only a senior science teacher, however posh had been Crofton House school, rather than a full-fledged biochemist. One, moreover, who had winged her way from British Columbia to both Yale and Columbia, then sampling a few European venues, and including a spell at Caltech in Pasadena before tiring of endless blue skies and deciding to return to the University of British Columbia for the sunset of her career.

When Deborah had settled herself on one of Geraldine's amply covered garden sofas and her hostess had brought them both stiff scotches—as usual minus either ice or soda water—she eased back to listen to why her friend had phoned her at such an early hour (it was not yet ten o'clock) and to let her get the theme of interfering family off her chest.

Geraldine did just that. It was only afterwards that things took a distinct change in tone and custom. Looking through the bottom of her empty tumbler (Deborah had only just started her drink) the old lady suddenly said "Debby, do you think I am the senile old fool that Hugh thinks? Or the evil bitch that my granddaughter sees?"

It wasn't that her friend was in any doubt as to the answer she was expected to give, but she knew that a merely polite negation, a mindless gesture of sentimental agreement, would drive her exacting friend to immediate wrath—not to mention a spate of further drinks that would by no means facilitate intelligent conversation.

"To start with, it's a matter of *wave lengths,* isn't it, Geraldine," she began. "They really haven't a clue about where—what you stand for, do they?" Deborah had been about to say "where you're coming from," but very often her prickly friend took umbrage at certain modernisms.

"Neither of 'em have the slightest idea where I'm coming from, Debby. Then my son's a male for one thing—and doctors of his ilk are still very circumscribed. As for that silly little Rebecca, even before she started on all that religious claptrap she was an ignorant girl. I always did think it a mistake to send her to York House rather than attend Crofton House as you and I did. Then my suspicion is that all her generation, regardless of schools, are barely literate, and have gained none of that knowledge that arises from sheer hard work."

Deborah closed her eyes. This was familiar territory.. She opened them quickly again, though, when her friend continued. "But lately I've been struggling with bigger things. *Dreams,* Debbie. I've been having the most horrible dreams. Sometimes I wake up in the middle of the night all of a sweat. It's then I'm not sure whether to try and sleep again—with the risk of returning to some ghastly situation where everything's against me—or to just lie there waiting for daylight or—who knows—maybe the end."

Deborah was already wracking her brains for something apposite to say. But she needn't have worried. Geraldine hadn't finished. "I'm thinking more about death these days, Deb. Not that I'm afraid of it or anything like that. I've never had problems with mortality—not since childhood. I just want it to be *right,* that's all. Short of an unexpected accident, it will just be the patched up ticker— what's left of it—giving out. I wouldn't have lived as long as I have if the old bod wasn't in relatively good shape. But I really would like to grow cold with a bit of dignity. Not slumped over the can or anything like that. No, it's the *social* aspects that bother me. They're the things that come into my dreams."

Deborah felt it time to say something but these were hazardous waters. Her own thoughts of her future demise took a far different course. But then as she humbly told herself so often, this woman was a titan compared with her. That brain never ceased working; part, indeed most, of Geraldine's loneliness stemmed from the gap she had ineluctably created between herself and the vast majority of her fellows.

"I'm not sure, Geraldine, I understand quite what you mean by "the social aspects." Could you amplify that for me?"

The old lady was used to that kind of question from a lifetime of lecturing and explaining her discoveries in the lab to her peers. She smiled genially at her friend. "The trouble is, Debby, that the rest of the world has NOT come to terms with leaving it. In spite of a lot of jabber about death being as natural as birth people either don't believe in death for a minute other than as a dire misfortune — or they refuse to think about it at all! I can't do that. I can't stop sifting and sorting and jabbing at everything that arrives at my mental door– even though, apart from precious you, my love, there isn't much more than Mr. Ballantine's blessed potion to really talk to."

Whether it was the small portion of that "blessed potion" that she had consumed, or the strength of that lovely April day, or just the odd sense of power that Geraldine's confidence in her common sense and honesty imposed upon her, Deborah took the bull by the horns.

"Of course, no one can share your ninety-six-year-old self, Geraldine. You're the pioneer there, just as you were for all those years with your research, both things that come with a concomitant isolation. But you do make things a little harder than they perhaps need be." She looked at her companion, searching for signs of unrest.

"Go on," Geraldine coaxed, obviously welcoming her friend's efforts, even anticipating a novel degree of frankness.

"Well, the more you reveal your sense of other people's limitations—"

"Like Hugh accusing me of being a snob?"

"If you like. Though I wouldn't have put it that way. The more they fear you, the worse you'll pull out of them. My Great Aunt Mabel used to say that fearful people were the most dangerous people."

"Did she say that? My own mother used to say frightened folk were often *frightening* folk. Same thing, really."

Deborah decided to plough on. "It doesn't really matter, Geraldine. As—as long as you appreciate that you don't always bring the best out of people. I—I should hate to think it colours your time here at Mayfair. What you've done in life, what benefits you've brought all of us in terms of your genetic discoveries—well, you deserve a happy, a rich retirement."

"We'll forget the greeting card sentiments," said Geraldine, returning instinctively to her normal asperity. "Anything else?"

But her tone was still level, and that was enough for her friend, who felt that as she was already in the deep end there was little reason to retreat to the shallows.

"You might just try it as an experiment. I mean giving someone the benefit of the doubt—assuming the *best* motives rather than the *worst.*"

The suggestion was met with a heavy silence. It was time to lighten the mood. "Of course, my dear," Deborah continued, "I'm not talking about the absolute idiots like Mrs Solway and the new ones you rightly call the oafs, with that awful music they play. I could personally strangle them myself as I hear their din even more than you do. They're right next door to me, after all."

Geraldine ignored her friend's attempt at light-heartedness. She was now wearing the most peculiar expression, one that made her look almost childlike—that is if you discounted the white hair straggled over the pink scalp and the blotched skin. "An experiment, you say? Well, why not? I've really not got all that much to lose, have I?" She gave a funny little laugh, commensurate with the expression. "And I can cheat a bit. If that Rebecca has the nerve to call I'll tell her I've found the Lord Jesus and she's interrupting my prayers."

Deborah started to chuckle, then to laugh. Geraldine joined her. The two women sat there, their whole bodies convulsed and tears streaming, until the unexpected sound of a ship's siren way out in the Bay brought them to their feet and searching in vain for the source that, as two native Vancouverites, they both usually associated with fog.

Chapter Four

Enter Jeremy

It was as if the world was in conspiracy to hold Geraldine to her resolution. First it was a call from Molosovich in his basement apartment. Could he come and take away anything she might have for recycling? She had a ton of bottles which she'd been planning to unload on Rebecca to get rid of with her own stuff. But now she decided it would be a good thing both to show appreciation for the man's gesture and at the same time to let him see how her apartment was still quite livable and if not quite spic and span, certainly no threat to anyone's health through lack of hygiene or degree of squalor.

She didn't ask him to sit down, though feeling such an egalitarian gesture would merely make him uncomfortable. She did however, enquire over his relatives still living precariously in Pristina and when he grunted they continued to exist, unlike so many poor Serbs in the province of Kosovo, she turned her questions to his own well-being.

To say Anton Molosovich was surprised would be an understatement; he was both astonished and profoundly suspicious as to her motives. She was the only person since

he had arrived in Canada who had persisted in treating
him as a serf. To be sure she used plenty of pleases and
thank yous—but these were tagged to orders, not requests.

"Please *come up here at once. The toilet is acting up
again.*"

"*I do not wish to hear tittle-tattle from other occupants
of this building....*

"Thank you, *but leave a note in my mail box and* please
do not call me except over matters of extreme urgency."

If she hadn't been as old as the hills and frail enough
for a fart to blow away he wouldn't have put up with her
crap. Yet here she was, actually asking after his health. And
to the best of his knowledge—he again checked her expression and person—she hadn't gone completely nuts.

"I got big ache in neck. Doctor say it vertebrates. That
right word? Then I get pain here in stomach? Have to
watch food. Pain in groin too."

She was nodding in unison with every fresh com-
plaint. He took courage from that. "Then get headaches—
sometime all night. Maybe tumor? Who know! Go through
hell back there in old country. Maybe I pay now in this
one." He paused, his hypochondria needing a refill.

She took advantage of the moment. "There's someone
I'd like you to see, Anton.

A close colleague of mine out at UBC. Dr. Peter
Eichelbaum. He's what we call a physiologist—specializing
in the brain. We were in Brussels together when I picked
up the Maurice Petard Award at the Belgian Neurological
Institute. Excellent fellow. By all means say that Dr.
Butterfield here recommended you."

Now as it happened Anton Molosovich had at one
time or other been seen by a bevy of physiologists, among

a whole army of specialists attached to St. Paul's and Vancouver General Hospital as well as several at UBC. The latter had included the man she now mentioned. It was why he knew that her Peter Eichelbaum had retired in 1991, the same year he had arrived in B.C. with his catalogue of complaints from Kosovo. In fact said Eichelbaum had been the first Anton had found wanting—in being dismally incapable of understanding his English, let alone unable to identify his broad range of excruciating illnesses the length and breadth of his body. At any other time, the janitor would have triumphantly told the old woman that her "close colleague" was now also drawing his Senior's pension and quite out of the picture, but now he just nodded, thanked her, and left her apartment wobbling perilously as he sought to hold onto an enormous bag of empty bottles.

Geraldine had no sooner flopped herself down to recover from his visit when the phone went again, only this time indicating it was someone downstairs at the buzzer, waiting to be let into the building. She fleetingly wondered if she could sustain all this forced amiability as she picked up the instrument. If she had believed in prayer she would have made supplication that it wasn't her idiot grand-daughter again. It wasn't—though it was someone in close degree of consanguinity. Her other grandchild, Jeremy.

She immediately suspected he was an emissary of Hugh, but although it was true that he carried from his father the medications she had asked for, there was no message from her son with which to concur or disagree. Jeremy, it transpired quickly, was full of his own preoccu-pations. At the first hint of them, and recalling her new role of amiability, Geraldine hustled him to the balcony and sat herself down on her favourite chaise-longue.

"Please take a seat, Jeremy, wherever you like." She essayed at mild wit. "They're all free today. It's the deckchair man's day off!"

To be sure, she wanted to appear a kinder, more tender person—but not *that* much kinder or more tender!

Her grandson stared at her. He was wondering why the hell he'd been rash enough to come to her place. As he was already sitting down when she made the invitation he just assumed that she was just a little more nuts than when he'd last seen her. Not surprising, of course, considering her age. But his Dad had only mentioned her orneriness and not her losing her senses. Then he remembered why he was there—and was glad that he'd made the effort before she went really off her handle.

"I've already found a seat over here by the palm plant, Grandma," he told her. "And I'm glad they're free because I'm broke."

She was ready for that. "What a pity," she said, "because I am, too. I can't give you so much as a penny. This time of the month every bit of the body has been clamoring for funds. I've given to the heart people, the lungs, the kidneys, and, of course, the arthritis bunch who never let up—like the disease itself, of course."

"I didn't come here for your money. I've got Dad for that."

Believing her son to be a total skinflint, that intrigued her. But the new Geraldine forbore further questions. "Then what is it, Jeremy dear, that this poor old lady can do for you? I'm all ears."

He smiled to himself. As she'd gotten older and her hair thinner, so had her ears, once tucked away, taken on much greater prominence. The rounded pearl earrings she foolishly persisted on wearing, he thought, though small, certainly didn't help matters.

But he struck out in quite a different direction. "I really came for your advice. You once told me, Grandma—oh, I couldn't have been more than thirteen or fourteen—that if ever I found myself at a total loss I was to come to you. That's what grandmothers are for, you said."

Geraldine remembered the moment perfectly. Only he was more like seventeen than fourteen. His voice was high-pitched if husky, he hung about with a boy named Clarence, and he evinced a passionate interest in small mammals, particularly furry ones rather than the likes of hedgehogs and porcupines. It was then she was convinced he was gay.

"I do remember," she now told him. "I also think it was the occasion that your mother was about to leave your much older father and go off with that aeronautics engineer from Seattle. I think I also sensed that you were having trouble with your sexual identity. You were the right age, anyway."

"People have enough trouble telling their parents they're gay. With grandparents it's just that much harder."

"So you've waited an extra ten years or so to find out what I thought you were, all along. It was your father who kept telling me I was mistaken and then that silly sister of yours."

"Rebecca? But she knew all along. When we were in school together. She knew my first crush. I've never held anything back from her. I even borrowed her perfume."

"Not that. It's simply that she's asked me to pray for you with her. What as a child she knew was perfectly natural for you, she now sees in her garbled mind as a perversion and the source of all your problems. Frankly, in my book, it's she who has the problems. You're just having trouble coming out. Belatedly, I may say. I had colleagues who were doing it better than you back in the Fifties when I was at Yale. There was Gerry Cesaretti in Microbiology. Mind you, he didn't have my Hugh as a father."

Jeremy sighed. This was proving even harder than he'd thought "It's not my coming out, Gran. Not even my break up with William. It's—it's what the hell am I going to do with my life?" The effort of that forced a sob from him and she looked up sharply. The atmosphere had changed, become suddenly darker. She caught his anguish, what she sensed was despair. It struck her in parts she had thought long closed.Now she was facing him. Abandoned was both the mask of irony she wore as normal armor nowadays, and the newly willed *douceur* that Deborah had suggested.

"What is it child? What's the matter?"

His response did more than puzzle her. It alarmed her profoundly. "I'm lost, Grandma. I don't know who I am or what I am. I don't know where I'm going. If William commits suicide as he keeps threatening I know it will be my fault. I think there's some kind of curse over me. I think deep down I'm evil."

"Now you're sounding just like that sister of yours," the old lady muttered, wondering what kind of taint was there in her descendants and horrified at the passive acceptance of this grandson's so passive claim to be rudderless, evil, and without any positive aim in life.

It was everything she was not, the ultimate blasphemy against her personal credo of a total focus of her goal as a woman and her passion for precision which underpinned the sacred vocation of the scientist. Even her son—and again, as always, she felt a tremor of guilt over his domestic upbringing—was a medical man, trained for accurate observation and the single-minded goal of health. What dreadful thing, then, had happened between him and his two offspring? She found hard to ascribe major blemishes on his seed to the half-witted woman he had so regrettably and belatedly elected to take as his wife.

But Jeremy had more confession to offer. He had the strongest feeling that this opportunity to pour his heart out before the matriarch of the family and who must surely herself, be close to death, would not be repeated. And he had had an awareness ever since he had entered her apartment that morning that she had changed, was somehow more like the kindhearted grandmother of fiction he had thought all other children happily possessed—rather than the shriveled ball of energy he had known since infancy, a cold being full of dynamic purpose to whom kids like himself were an irrelevancy, cloying impediments to the loftier purposes of life for those blessed with brains and who also had the courage to grasp the opportunities accorded them.

He looked afresh at her. He had taken a risk, prompted perhaps by desperation, and was now glad he'd done so. "I've always felt you despised me. And, do you know? deep down I agreed with you! Then to look at you was to look at the sun. It hurt the eyes. It numbed what apology I had for a brain. That's why whenever I tried to speak to you it came out as nonsense. It probably still does."

She refused to comment, not because she didn't wish to reassure, but because she, too, had the feeling that if he didn't speak the whole of his mind then and there, he never would.

"Just think, Grandma. Next month I'll be twenty-five. By then you not only had a couple of degrees, but had marked out your next university move and knew precisely whatever it was you were determined to be. And me? I dropped out of Simon Fraser, as you know. I failed as a lover, and I haven't held a job for more than six months at best. I hated all of 'em! Dad's supporting me at the moment—but that can't go on."

That did bring a confirmatory "no" from her. Nothing else, though. She was still waiting.

"I have just one thing left I think I'd like to try. But it's so off the wall that everyone will think I'm as dumb as ever. There are no prospects, a lousy salary I'm sure. I'm sure it will make the likes of you and Dad cross me right off your list. Besides, with my spotty CV I'm not sure I could even get the job."

"Your father and I are not one and the same but what in hell is the job anyway? An attendant on a space bus?"

He smiled faintly. "Nearly. I saw an ad in our local paper. It's for an attendant at the Greater Vancouver Zoo out in Langley. I've been there several times with people's kids like William's nieces and Cousin Leslie's little boy. I was really impressed. They are trying to make it a real zoological operation—not just a menagerie for children. There's already an excellent breeding program for endangered species that I think you'd approve of. And a proper classification with Latin names given, Gran," he added expressly for her benefit. He tried to read her bulbous eyes and decide whether her head was shaking from senility or approval. "I'd only be cleaning out stalls, a bit of grooming, that kind of thing. There's a miniature train for the kids and their parents and one of the keepers shouts out information as they pass the enclosures. That's about as high as I could get if I started at the bottom."

She looked at him, no, *stared* at him, her head wobbling as ever, but now a rare smile hinting at the extravagant wrinkles at the corners of her mouth.

"You know what, Jeremy? I think that's the best bloody suggestion I've heard in a month of Sundays." Then she thought of Debbie's advice for her the day before. "Well *one* of the best bloody suggestions. I think we should phone them right now. Do you have the number or shall I get Molosovich to find it?"

"I have it here." An excited Jeremy got up to use the phone. "Boy, am I glad I had the nerve to bring it up!"

"Sit down" she ordered. "I'll do the phoning. I'm not as confident about the *bona fides* of that place as you seem to be. They could very well be a commercial sham masquerading as scientifically legitimate. But we can at least try and see what a bit of name-dropping can do. They can't see what an old wreck I am, and this is still Vancouver, if I'm not mistaken."

Jeremy left her apartment a happy young man. Geraldine wanted to summon Debbie to celebrate her grandson's upcoming interview with a few scotches, but her wayward digestion called her once more for an extended period in the bathroom. She caught a glimpse of her massively wrinkled self in the floor length mirror before sitting down—and that not only blotted out her recent success with her grandson but made her depressed all over again.

Chapter Five

Entrance of Evil

It was hard, even though she strove to accomplish it, for Geraldine to live even a minimally unregulated life—given her age and the dictates of her body. In vain did she quaff her Ballantines to loosen the thongs of physical restriction, in vain did she call an old colleague in Melbourne, another retired back to Delhi, a third holed up and like herself, now professionally forgotten, in the Berkshires—to feed onetime extensive and personal horizons. She had even allowed Hugh to install a laptop and send a local cretin to instruct her usage of email and the worldwide web—an accomplishment which had taken her but three days of the paid "guru" for a week's instruction as she quickly grew to resent the man's total lack of imagination, and worse still, his patronizing treatment of her as a little old lady in need of pampering..

Although she had never come to love the technology, she made herself sit down with the computer—especially when the telephone started to ring and she was reluctant to answer in case it was Hugh or Rebecca, or some pestilential neighbor. Then she would hunt and peck (never having mastered typing) and tap out the address of some remote person—sadly, few of her contemporaries had adopted the device—and give them the benefit of her current views of the world, her detestation of any kind of feminism save her own, and ask of their accomplishments in their fields. These were mainly members of the bio-chemistry community as she rarely strayed from the men and women she thought of as sharing her own discipline. In any case, she felt that her branch of the sciences was the world which embraced the current horizons of human advance and those areas in which the species would be genetically saved or ultimately lost.

Geraldine's physical realm rarely extended as far as the view from her balcony. She had always perceived the attitude of Tennessee William's Blanche Dubois with her "reliance on the kindness of strangers" as an acceptance of male dominance and extended her refusal to rely on other people to both friends and acquaintances.

It was only when someone like Deborah Tregaskis made the suggestion and backed it up with soft and subtle persuasion, that she allowed herself to be escorted down the elevator to the foyer and down the broad flight of steps to the busy tree-lined avenue bordering the waters of English Bay.

Geraldine did not consider herself a particularly self-conscious woman but as she walked slowly and deliberately towards Stanley Park along what the Brit-born citizens called "the front", her hand on Debbie's arm in lieu of a stick, she found herself thinking she was out of place. Not because she was the only ancient person out there enjoying the massed beds of tulips and pansy borders, but because such factors were reminders of spring and the birth of a new year. 'Whereas I'm a reminder to all of them of winter and…. ?' she thought to herself—while all the time talking quite differently to her unsuspecting friend.. "The sun's nice and warm on the skin," was what she was saying. "And I can now say it is responsible for all my freckles, can't I?"

Deborah's mind was elsewhere. She was thinking how fortunate she was to have struck up a friendship with her current companion. It had been soon after she had bought her apartment and in a chance chat at the mail box they had discovered that they'd both been girls at Crofton House—even though some years apart. She was well aware that her affection for Geraldine was not shared by the other inhabitants of Mayfair Lodge. And, from what her old friend had told her, that negative opinion was shared by at least two of Geraldine's immediate relatives—indeed, three until the recent transformation of her grandson from skeptic to admirer.

Nor had Geraldine ever attempted to soften or divert the comments of her detractors. It had taken several months before Deborah had realized that the occupant of Apt.# 2705 was largely unconcerned about such people; her irritation was much more involved with the receding tide of recognition of her scientific achievements over half a century. She very often had to make a blunt statement as to what she had fought for as a woman, what she had achieved—all of which made life so meaningless if not humiliating.

It hadn't always been like that, of course, as Geraldine had carefully informed Debbie. There'd been all those honors… the usual doctorates from major universities the world wide; the prestigious Wittenstern Award for Pioneer Work in Microbiology, the Van Leiden Medal for Scientific

Research, and, her own favorite, her election to Membership of The Royal Society.

Geraldine's professional peers in the international scientific world had never been less than lavish with their praise and had continued to lavish praise upon her. (Oh yes, she was aware of the fawners and brown-noses too!) until their numbers had been gradually diminished by death.

Death...Debbie's recollection of her friend's pleasures and peeves of her friend gave out when she arrived at such finality. She who so easily grew restless at thoughts of her own demise, of how *soon* it would be, what *guise* it would come in, how *sustained* would be her departure. Death was something—one of the very few topics—that she didn't feel like bringing up with Geraldine, fearing her scorn and mockery. She knew her friend would duck the fact of her own great age and emphasize that, for a retired science school mistress from Crofton House, a death at seventy-one or two would be a perfectly congruous matter, an appropriate age for her farewell, especially as there were still multitudes about who had respected Deborah Tregaskis as a colleague and, even more, those who had loved her as their teacher.

No, her musings on death, she was sure, would find no sympathy from that ear with a large pearl attached to it, belonging to the frail and stooped figure who was currently using her in lieu of a walking stick.

How wrong she was! At that very moment, Geraldine was brooding on how remote she felt in the exhaustion of her days to the throng that pulsated about her. Out there in the open air, where the world teemed, she was suddenly keenly aware of the barrier her years set up between her and the racial mix of youths, mostly Chinese and Caucasian, sprawled on the grassy banks that led down to the sand and sea. She felt cut off from those sauntering to and fro past the elderly couple, their unwrinkled faces bubbling over with laughter and smiles while they talked of a thousand things that would never again bear much relevance for her or Debbie.

If Geraldine had been prone to depression—which she wasn't—she might well have been saddened then by that sense of isolation. While Debbie mused sadly over her own sense of being walled up by the years, her companion knew only a degree of anger, or perhaps frustration, at her comparable plight. But even that was not designed to last long, for as Geraldine pursed lips and scowled at those who in their callow indifference threatened to bump into the two of them, she saw a ghost. At least before she started to think rationally, (a rare moment of unbridled emotion) she was convinced she saw a ghost.

It was Dr. Peter Eichelbaum she saw, the same man she had recommended just one month earlier to her building's janitor as a brilliant specialist in physiology and who someone—for the life of her she couldn't remember who—had more recently informed her had succumbed to cancer after a long struggle. She hadn't informed Molosovich—or anyone else for that matter—of their one-time close relationship—the word *torrid* occurred to her as she now saw him standing there after emerging from an apartment building across the busy road—that had developed between them after the shared professional experience in Belgium and the discovery they were booked into the same hotel.

Geraldine's love-life, apart from the abortive experience with Hugh's father (which she had soon dismissed as disastrous and from which she rapidly eliminated sex) had been meager. After that non-stop weekend with the lust-filled Peter, the affair waned quickly—and soon after the advent of menopause, her sex life became non-existent. Nor was she disposed to relive those sexual experiences and only once, after an impressive number of downed scotches, was she drawn to discuss any of them with her equally sex-restrained friend, Debbie.

It was that recent conversation that leaped to the fore of Geraldine's mind, even as her last lover's name raspingly but quite loudly escaped her scrawny throat. She hoped that her description of Peter had not been so graphic that Deborah would now recognize the man who now turned towards the curb and stared in her direction. But then Peter was dead and the man was a ghost. Debbie wouldn't even see him! Why, then, did she quicken and return Geraldine's grasp? What was her attention focused on if not the old man, waving slightly as he peered, seeming bewildered, across the pavement as the cars buzzed by, to where the two women stood? She was probably looking past them to the beautifully manicured lawn bowling greens in the park, where Debbie loved to bowl with the other white-clad figures, mostly seniors, and where they were duly headed now as spectators

As it happened, nothing was as Geraldine thought. But there was a savage interruption before the truth emerged. She did not scream his name a second time but no matter. He had already left the curb and begun to weave in her direction. She saw no vehicle bearing down on him. Nor, obviously, did he see the RV hurtling towards the entrance to the park.

Like a movie run in slow motion, she saw a bundle of splayed legs and white hair, thrown right up onto the hood, slither and then fall crumpled at the road's median where a second car had to swerve sharply not to run right over the huddled body. As if of one mind, the two elderly women risked the traffic coming from the opposite direction and, with Debbie holding up one arm to prevent further carnage, they arrived at the motionless figure from which a thin, dark flow sought the gentle camber of the pavement before starting to trickle towards the curbside drain. Other figures began to run towards them. But Geraldine was heedless of the commotion. The white faced, mustached old man she was staring down at was no ghost. Nor was it Peter Eichelbaum. The body bore not a remote resemblance to her suitor of half a century earlier.

She was about to kneel down to check his pulse and breath, she was secretly glad when a younger woman, announcing she was a doctor, did just that. After that, the woman righted herself and made her grave announcement. Geraldine had known he was dead—couldn't escape the sense she had known he was dead when that damned RV had struck him. Worse, was full of the even grimmer import that it was her hoarsely calling out the name of Peter that had begun the last few moments of the unknown's life.

She felt a tug on her sleeve and turned away from the bloody form to face a crying Debbie. Geraldine sought to comfort her friend but over and over in her tired old head played the refrain: *I was the harbinger of his death. Perhaps that's the only real power I have left.*

Chapter Six

Email Exchange

Geraldine rarely printed out her equally rarely received emails; she considered it a waste of paper. Most of them were in response to one of hers and therefore abusive, so she quickly consigned them to the *permanent deletion* her computer indicated. But she reserved particular bile for the author of an email enquiry asking whether she was the recipient of a Science Council of British Columbia award recognizing her contribution to the provincial scientific community. Unfortunately she misread or misunderstood the address at the top of the communication and made the assumption that it came from the Council itself. She had forgotten the small plaque, honoring her election as a member of the Council and dated 1972 when she was 65, that lay collecting dust and buried with a pile of others also long forgotten. Now the misunderstood email served to fuel her conviction that she was not only ignored but had never been properly recognized.

She had emailed the enquirer as follows:

Dear Whoever-you-are (I can't make sense of all that

damn address jargon)

If your organization were as competent as its title is pompous you would know that I have never been contacted by your bunch—let alone been given some stupid award. It sounds the kind of thing that dentists and veterinarians prize but is of no particular consequence to someone working in my restricted field of microbiology. I have a friend who is a retired science teacher here in Vancouver and I will enquire from her if she has ever heard of you lot and whether she has been honoured with whatever it is you hand out. Am I to presume that you restrict your patronage to women? I don't know where on earth you got my name, unless it was in random from the telephone directory. But if you ever embark on anything like records you might look in the recent Encyclopedia of British Columbia *where, my friends tell me, you will find my name and such relevant data as my membership of The Royal Society, the Van Leiden Medal for Scientific Research, and The Maurice Petard Award. You might also check* The Canadian Encyclopedia *which has a page or two on me.*

Sincerely—Geraldine Butterfield, Dr. Sc. Prof Emeritus Etc.

She was rather surprised, then, to receive that very same day a further missive from presumably the same source—only this time revealing the author was one Paul D. Wong and that rather than belonging to any scientific organization he was a free-lance journalist who had met her grandson at The Greater Vancouver Zoo and would very much like to visit and interview her for a long article he wished to write on famous Canadian women pioneers.

Geraldine's reply was considerably warmer, if still a little cautious.

Dear Paul Wong: I do appreciate alacrity in correspon-

dence and familiarity with my extremely gifted grandson gives me yet more confidence. Although quite elderly, I am still very busy with both telephone enquiries and, of course, email correspondence such as yours. However, I am sure we can come up with a mutually convenient time. If you came for coffee or something I could manage a subsequent sand-wich—with something to wash it down. I should add that I would really require precision and accuracy with my scientif-ic accomplishments that have extended over many years. Needless to say, a career like mine invariably results in mak-ing enemies and detractors as well as admirers –given human nature with its reservoir of jealousy, envy, hatred, and greed, as well as the more admirable qualities. If you should decide to telephone me here at 0-604-921-9326 then please let the phone ring at least five times as I do not answer immediate-ly—for the same reasons I have just given over those bent on ensuring my day is a less than happy one.

Yours very sincerely—Geraldine Butterfield.

Such was the background to the downstairs phone call announcing the arrival of Paul David Wong. Paul was in his early twenties and born in Victoria as were his par-ents; his grandparents having arrived in the B.C. capital as young immigrants from mainland China. He was thus thoroughly Canadian of the westcoast variety, but never-theless inheriting that innate respect for the elderly which remains a hallmark of Chinese culture—after all else, including politeness, has been subsumed into brusque North American life generally and westcoast casualness in particular. Not that there was anything obsequious about the young man's attitude towards her—Geraldine would have soon erupted over that—but somehow incorporated into his wholly egalitarian attitude (which suggested an almost cheeky approach delivered in a clear but fast-paced voice) was the kind of respect Anglo Saxons only offered ancient institutions and ruins and which to the diminutive and venerable scientist, was something refreshingly new.

It came up right from the start. "You got a nice place here. Nothing starchy and with a decent lived-in look. That your Mom and Dad?"

Geraldine was astonished. The slim, if quite tall, boy (judging from her grandson's height she guessed this one was a good six foot) had managed to weave himself between the irregular stockpiles of furniture to reach an otherwise half-hidden escritoire which had on its surface a single photo stuck slightly askew in the middle of a line of miscellaneous objects. They'd been collected on her numerous academic expeditions and now served not so much as spurs to memory as the resting place for dust.

The photo he had already picked up and blown on heavily was indeed of her father and mother. The one time surveyor was wearing a top hat and frock coat that would have rendered him eligible for Queen Victoria's Diamond Jubilee, while his spouse nestled close to him, was draped entirely in black—an atramentous veil flowing down from her large-brimmed hat to the full-length ink-black dress with its pleated cape. From what one could see of her face, and certainly the whole of his, their joint expressions were set in a grim scowl. Geraldine dimly recalled that her parents had been attending a funeral when the photograph was taken. But neither Isabella nor Horatio Butterfield had enjoyed the threats to privacy of a camera and only submitted to them when they felt that special duty called.)

"They don't seem too happy," said Paul.

"In those days it was not considered a duty to wear a

sickly grin for photos," countered Geraldine.

"Bully for them!" said her visitor, before setting the photo carefully back down on the lines the dust had created for it, and moving sinuously forward between a non-functioning grandfather clock and a Shaker rocking chair acquired during her Eastern Seaboard days. The rocking chair was piled with books and faced towards the greater pool of daylight and wider degree of space proximate to the plate glass windows.

"I bet you aren't afraid of anyone breaking in here," he remarked. "A bit less light and they'd break their necks. Good idea," he added. "Specially because I bet you know every inch you can get around in between all the books stacked up by the walls. And judging by the little bit I've just seen, Dr. Butterfield, you've lived a lot and read twice as much again. I just know you've got a wonderful story to tell. Gosh, I'm glad I took Jeremy's advice and got up enough nerve to email you in the first place!"

Honed in suspicion though she well might be, Geraldine was not wholly immune to such genial comment. "There are those," she said dryly, "who have likened my rather casual display of things to the ménage of Miss Havisham—as enumerated by Dickens in his *Great Expectations.*" She grew uncomfortably aware that his plaudits were making her wordy. '*Prolix*' sprang to mind—though that was something she usually only extolled in contemptuous comparison when encountering the word-anemic young who also perverted their speech by inflecting the last word of each sentence with a note of interrogation, making every statement sound like an idiotic question.

This Paul Wong, though, was free of that particular

vice. Indeed he seemed singularly liberated from a great number of the shortcomings embraced by the contemporary young. For instance, the cuffs of his windbreaker stopped at his wrists. His trousers were not mere bags of voluminous material (enough for two bums in most pairs of pants, she'd observed) which flopped over enormous white rubber shoes before brushing the ground. His hair was neither spiky nor frizzed, bright green or orange, but salutary straight and Chinese black. And he continued to address her as if she were really present, a person of consequence whose presence he was grateful to share. He was proving rather a dear boy in fact.

She allowed herself to wonder if he'd known any *dalliance* with her Jeremy. Followed that by a determination to delicately find out and, if such was not the case, to try her hand as an admittedly rather dilapidated Cupid. He even readily concurred in drinking a Scotch with her, smacking his lips and pronouncing it elixir. (Though that was somewhat duplicitous as he covertly decided it tasted like cat's piss which was his designation for all gustatory hates, beginning with an idiosyncratic if lifelong one for a Chinese lad—cilantro.)

They started the interview with a shared childhood in Victoria, his technique being to make an observation about something in his own life (his widowed grandmother had owned a grocery store) and then asking how her own girlhood had been different. This took them away from anything like a Q&A routine and suited Geraldine much better as she was disposed to dilate on anything that took her fancy.

She was doing that very thing when she broke off. "Before I go into our move to Kerrisdale when Father took a position in Engineering at UBC, hadn't you better start writing things down? You seem bright enough but when I get to Crofton House, things will get more complicated."

With a little flourish, Paul opened his jacket: revealed a miniature tape recorder strung across part of his pant's belt. "State of the art," he declared. "Super mike that picks up everything."

Geraldine made no specific response. If it were similarly placed on her, she ruefully reflected, the rebellious noises of her stomach would have drowned out anything as feeble as a human voice.

"Just wanted to make sure," she said. "Now I can get on to the Sapphic influences I encountered at Crofton House."

Her abrupt frankness made gay Paul suddenly as keen to be honest as she was being. "Your glass is nearly empty," he said. "Why don't you have a fill up." He paused fractionally. "I won't have another of those as they're a bit strong for me. Would you have a gin and tonic by any chance?"

He was surprised that for someone of her advanced age and shakiness, she had the agility to slide off the crisscrossed strips of plastic covering her metal-framed chaise longue as she announced she was just nipping inside to retrieve the Schweppes from the fridge. She added over her shoulder that he'd find the bottle of gin in the disused parrot cage (a disappointing present from son Hugh at her initial retirement when she'd rejected its feathered inhabitant) just beyond where they were both sitting.

When they resumed conversation and she had covered the wiles and designs of Louise Bedford and Joan Weatherspoon (two fellow Twelfth Graders), in some detail over the Lesbian experiments enacted between the three of them, she suddenly turned the talk away from Crofton in the 1920s to more recent times and the likes of himself and her grandson.

"I don't profess to be an authority in these matters, Paul, but am I right in thinking that you and Jeremy hit it off in a very special way, out there at the zoo?"

Paul was halfway there but not *quite* prepared for the speed of her frontal assault.

"We found we are both crazy about the Kermode bear—you know the white one, *Ursus Americanus Kermodei*? There is an orphaned cub at the zoo and I came across Jeremy when they first let him feed it with the formula bottle. It turns out that we both have studied the spirit or snow bear. Jeremy says he can identify with a sub-species."

An unsatisfied Geraldine sniffed. "You seem to have the *nomenclature* off pat. Can you be as precise about you and Jeremy?"

Obstinacy knows no age limits. "I'd love to talk more about Jeremy, Dr. Butterfield, but I'm sure you'll understand I must stick to you and my book" (Upping his task from a mere article). "I'm free-lance you see. I have a grant but it won't last unless I get a fair amount done every day. On a later visit, perhaps? Maybe I could come with your grandson?"

Geraldine wasn't exactly mollified but she recognized steel when she met it.

"Who else is going to be in this—this *book*?"

That was a question to which Paul had a practiced response. "Well, let me see, there's already Ivy Brumage the City Planner in Halifax, and Helen Gurney Blasche, probably the most famous glass artist out of Ontario in her day. They're both already in the bag. And Dr. Wilma Hayworth has promised an interview—she was the first woman electrical engineer graduate out of the University of Saskatchewan—and I musn't forget Dr. Ida Hart the anthropologist from Victoria who wrote the famous *Apes in Petticoats*—she's also agreed. Then I've also contacted Marie-Lorraine Demarais in Quebec, the leading Canadian authority on tundra -"

"That's enough, for the moment. But I think you need some real scientists like myself. Not just anthropologists and, worse, sociologists." Then rather ambiguously, Geraldine added: "If the holes in the net are too wide the fish escape."

He wasn't about to pick that one up. "Of course, you are the star of the collection. You will give it a gravity and an historical importance that it otherwise couldn't have. When I mentioned your name to my potential editor he was thrilled to bits."

"We have reached the university and my first experience of the male conspiracy to keep us women in our place. By the by, I shall name names as all the bastards are now dead." She took such a swig from her tumbler he expected her to splutter. Instead she merely held up her glass enquiringly, and quick-witted Paul immediately jumped up to replenish it from the bottle by her side.

"You will help yourself as and when," she murmured, nodding what he took as approval of his act but aware that her head hadn't stopped its rhythmic bobbing since his arrival.

"I don't want to miss a single case of your famous fights with *the patriarchy*," he announced. "Jeremy mentioned several and it is time the whole world was made aware." He was speaking slightly louder than was his custom but it didn't seem to bother her. Perhaps she was even deafer than she'd suggested, he thought. In any case she just smiled dreamily, even as she continued to nod. "I had many glorious *battles* with them wot got *tassels,*" she announced as if quoting a poem. "And I shall deliver them to you *seriatim.*"

She was as good as her word. In fact Paul had to pay a second visit and by the close of that hadn't got beyond Geraldine's first year as a grad student at UBC and her first interest in comparative ophthalmology fired quite oddly (if now prophetically) by her work on the disparity of sight and hearing in the black bear. Then part of that session had been spent in fending off her enquiries about himself and a discussion she would evidently relish over prospects for her grandson as a zoologist. She had in mind images of Sir Julian Huxley, FRZS, whom she'd met at his Hampstead home in London—but she wasn't disposed to tell her young biographer that. Not yet, at least…

Paul had left her on that second occasion both satisfied and frustrated.

Chapter Seven

Decisions! Decisions!

Geraldine had never, ever, thought of herself as a procrastinator, but her friend, Deborah gently suggested that she was perhaps becoming one. Geraldine's response was to threaten to take away the apartment key that she had given her neighbour just a few days earlier. The only person, as Geraldine had already asseverated so many times subsequently, on whom she had bestowed such a singular act of trust and confidence that her privacy would never be violated.

Deborah, having let herself into the crowded living room after phoning to say she was on her way, not only remained adamant after the lengthy telephone disagreement that had preceded her visit, but took it one degree forward.

"Darling," she said, voice as dulcet as ever, "you are not only putting off a very basic decision but I think you are denying *why* you're doing it. If I'm wrong I'll buy you a crate of Ballantines' or leap from your balcony—whichever you prefer."

"At least you've made me thirsty with your ridiculous

talk," came the reply—followed by the old lady's instant turning of her back and disappearing momentarily behind her mounds of books and furniture and repairing quickly if unsteadily to her cache of Scotch.

"I suppose you'll grumble that it's far too early for me to imbibe," she said, when starting to do just that." I keep forgetting you were a Cornish Methodist or something."

"It isn't nine o'clock yet, Geraldine." Deborah spoke neutrally, determined not to be sidetracked by a much older argument between them. "But I'll have a dollop in my coffee if it's all the same to you." She decided to pursue the initial conversation then and there, even as she pursued her old friend's humped back towards the kitchen. At least she wasn't going to be elusive as Geraldine had become recently. As soon as they were sitting facing each other, listening to the rain hitting the glass of the screen doors, she began, "I think you should come for a walk with me when it clears up. It would do you good—better than being cooped up here all the time."

"Cooped up? You make me sound like some battery-housed chicken. Do I have to remind you I have the sun and fresh air every time I step out on that balcony? As for exercise—I'm to and fro from that bloody bathroom twenty-four hours a day! I 'm walking now more than when I was working at The Radcliffe Infirmary in Oxford and had to walk miles between the lab and my office—let alone my rooms in Lady Margaret Hall."

"It's not the same."

"What's not the same?"

"Then and now."

Deborah could almost feel her friend bristle. She pushed on nevertheless. "It's to do with that car accident isn't it? That old man being killed. I know it is however you try and deny it. You haven't been the same from that day to this. I don't know what's eating you, Geraldine, but something made you afraid. You keep telling me that you're not afraid of death—well, now I'm not so sure." She rested. If that wasn't Geraldine bait she didn't know what was.

Ninety-six years of restless energy plunked herself down on the nearest armchair with such force that a cloud of dust rose about her. Deborah decided that when this battle between them was over she must turn again to the one involving a daily cleaning woman—perhaps one who combined nursing skills—rather than the scared rabbit who appeared once every two weeks and was out of the place in less than a couple of hours.

"You don't understand even a little bit, my dear Debbie. You haven't even reached the gap between seventy and ninety—let alone crossed it. You are closer to my son than me and I'm closer to an Egyptian mummy!"

"Not the way you jumped into that chair!"

Geraldine ignored that. They both were well versed now in the rules of the game. "It's my *pins*, ninny. I'm too unsteady on my pins to risk out there. What happened to him could happen to me. And watched by all those gaping kids, on top of it. That thought alone revolts me. They'd all come rushing up to help a dear old lady and treat a body devoid of a brain. It's obscene..

"You'd have me. Just like always. Since when haven't I been there for you to lean on? That was understood right off the bat. Right from the first time we went out together. Do you think for a minute I'd let you down? Now *that's* an obscene thought. No, Geraldine, you've suffered a sea change and that's what you're not telling me."

But Geraldine wasn't about to share her ghost. Even when her lips were white with death she was determined that the name Peter Eichelbaum would not pass between them. "I'll admit that accident—well mildly upset me. I'm just not in the mood for sustained perambulation, that's all."

Debbie changed her tack. When Geraldine invoked words like 'perambulation' it was merely another sign of her obduracy. "O.K. so you don't want to walk along the street with me. Would you trust me as a chauffeur? My car's in tip-top condition and I've never gotten a ticket."

The notion suddenly appealed to Geraldine. It not only got her off the hook over further walks with her friend but seemed a perfect solution to another problem that had been occupying her—that was how to join Jeremy and young Paul Wong on an expedition to the Greater Vancouver Zoo without exposure to the driving of either. She was deeply skeptical of the prowess of all the younger generation with respect to autos. It was what had made her prevaricate twice to the urging of Paul when he'd called her.

She bent forward. "There's something you could do—only I don't want to take advantage of your good nature, Debbie."

Debbie knew she'd sort of won one battle—even if she was about to be used by her wicked old friend in some elaborate scheme of which she might never learn the whole. "Fire away," she said resignedly. "Where do you want to go?"

"It's in aid of my grandson, Jeremy," Geraldine began. "I told you I managed to get him a job at that zoo? Well, I think I can be of use in his personal life as well. But I'd certainly need your help, Debbie. I need you as what they call *wheels*."

Deborah didn't hesitate. She knew that the important thing for Geraldine was psychological rather than physical—to get her out of that crowded apartment from which she'd refused to budge for now nearly two weeks. "And where would you like those *wheels* to go?"

Geraldine both knew and enjoyed the fact that she was about to employ her skills at cunning. After all, it was one of the few mental tests left to her. "I'm not quite sure, dear. In fact I was going to ask you to help me in that quarter. For a start, I'd like you to meet my biographer—well, the young man writing the thing on me for his *Canadian Encyclopedia of Woman Pioneers*. I think he can be of considerable help to Jeremy and as he's the only member of my family I've any respect for, that would mean so much to me. How about it, eh?"

That didn't give Deborah much time to think. But as a matter of fact she had already taken some steps vis-à-vis Paul D. Wong and knew far more about him than Geraldine could have ever suspected. The latter having dropped a clue as to his scheduled second visit, Deborah bearded him in the corridor and, having reassured the startled young Chinese writer that she was Geraldine's intimate companion, promised him she'd fill in the blanks that she knew her devious friend would leave in any account she might duly offer him.

"I'd be happy to do that, Geraldine," she said. "Just let me know when he's coming here next and I can arrange to be home too."

That information naturally allowed her to intercept

Paul as he stepped out of the elevator and tell him swiftly that she was to be invited into Geraldine's to meet him and that their hostess would then unfold her plan for the three of them and Jeremy, which would involve the use of her and her car.

The three of them, so diverse in ages, backgrounds, and current motives, successfully lied when each deemed it necessary and terminated their initial gathering feeling fondly about the other two and each contentedly, if falsely, sensing that they'd gotten their own way...

Chapter Eight

Voyage Into Someone's Truth

Deborah wasn't too happy about Geraldine's arrangement but there was little she could do about it. She had used the word "chauffeur" when offering her help to her friend and the old lady had insisted upon a literal translation. So while Deborah sat alone up front and at the wheel of her 1989 Volvo sedan, Geraldine and Paul were closeted in back.

Nor was Deborah all that happy about one or two other things issuing from Geraldine's seating plan. The first of these could hardly be laid at her friend's door. Neither age nor car manufacturer was responsible for the difficulty in making conversation between the front and back seats of automobiles. That problem abetted by the fact that none of the three, stemming from the impediments of age (Geraldine and Deborah) to temperament (Paul)—were disposed to shout, let alone yell, to sustain conversation.

But looming yet larger was Geraldine's determination to keep her friend from hearing all of what she intended to say to the young man during the trip and, perhaps equally,

DAVID WATMOUGH

her hankering to frustrate the friend who, acts of kindness aside, was in a word, snoopy—something else Geraldine put down to Debbie's Cornish ancestry and Methodist upbringing. At least, that was her silent reasoning for not having Paul sit up front. But there was also perhaps an old lady's reluctance to sit in isolation because so much of her home life was spent thus. Added to these factors was the vague if persistent desire to be naughty, to be the nasty little *shit-stirrer* her brother, Stuart, had been wont to call her when sitting in back with him in their Dad's Olds.

The thought of her brother triggered an ancient memory of a trip taken some eighty years earlier when they were visiting the Hudson's Bay compound at Fort Langley and therefore traveling in the same direction but on a now vanished country road.

As Debbie's car left the confines of the city and entered the multi-lanes of the TransCanada Highway a sudden sense of isolation engulfed her. How vast was the divide between her and her companions, how impossible the chance of throwing a line of communication across all that accumulation of separated experience.

She might score off Deborah, succeed in a nice little tit-for-tat for her irritating bossiness as they sat alongside each other on the tubular lounge chairs on her balcony in The Mayfair Apartments pretending a unity that could not be. But that puny reward didn't compensate for the fact that whenever she tried to blur the disparity of age between them, attempt what in her day had been called "girl talk" (or even essay comparison between their basic sexual adventures, which were surely, she felt, beyond the taint of history), Geraldine could never rid herself of the impression that what escaped from prudish Debbie as callow and

60

embarrassing confessions, emerged from her own mouth as merely quaint. A little bit of yesterday which should have been left to rest under last fall's leaves.

She shifted in her seat from the embarrassment of it. There had been nothing "quaint" about the ugly antics of her drunken husband, Walter, the night he hit her for refusing to attend that stupid formal dinner with him at Rutgers in New Jersey. She'd refused because he had declined to accompany her to nearby Princeton when she was being honoured for her early work on nucleotides. That had been back in 1942 during World War II, long before the double helix theory had been announced by Watson and Crick in 1953. Their son, Hugh, had been begotten in the fleeting and reluctant reconciliation which had concluded that particular row. His upbringing as a marital pawn, she willingly conceded, had taken place in the sustained reverberation from Walter's quasi rape of her that obscene night of conception. Nor did the word *quaint* bear the slightest relevance to a single moment she had subsequently spent with Peter Eichelbaum, the last brief glow in that truncated series of erotic experiences which constituted her time taken out as a *female* of the species, those relatively brief, if sometimes messy, moments stolen from the harsh excitement of winning her way to the pinnacles of her profession.

She looked across at Paul. Took in the unblemished Chinese skin, the still visible hints in the soft facial curves of his youth. With him, though, time took yet another twist. Not the sheer discrepancy between *their* ages but in what he stood for in the march of human progress. This she found harder to clothe in words but the sense of division was just as real. It had to do with gayness. His gayness.

No, she chided herself, she was being too severe on the young man. For it was something she had encountered intermittently throughout her career but which had gathered momentum and grown in ubiquity in the years after WW II and which revealed itself in a whole generation of queer young men—there were few outspoken dykes then—as they became emboldened, spoke of gay pride, and sounded as if the major socio-political achievement of the times was Gay Liberation.

That had always been hard for her to take. After all, it was *women*—not a tiny percentage of the race who were inverts but the goddamned gender *majority!*—as far back as the first flickering years of the century—who had gone into battle for their rights, and faced prison and humiliation on a grand scale before the enemy had crumbled. Their bastions been occupied. Only then were the likes of Dr Geraldine Butterfield, FRS, able to insist on the fully realized potential of their being.

Not that for one moment, she now argued, did she deny or show hostility to homosexual rights—to the contrary—but Dr. Butterfield felt that for far too many of these *gentle* men there was lacking a proper sense of proportion. Part of her insistence on the seating arrangements in Debbie's car was motivated by her intention to see that this wasn't the case with Master Paul Wong. That is before they all met up with her grandson and she could ascertain the contours and quality of the bonds between this witty, ambitious young man, and her own immature and thus vulnerable Jeremy.

Geraldine recalled her eager rationalization over her husband's insensitivity to her talents and career; and the *Sturm und Drang that* had caused—and was determined that as far as she was concerned there'd be nothing like the same kind of willed ignorance and striving to destroy the other's career between these two young men. Nothing to damage whatever relationship they sought and that she might help them to construct as they confronted their twenty-first century future.

"What do you think of Jeremy's prospects at The Greater Vancouver Zoo?" she began." I know I asked you that before but I want a more detailed answer this time."

After two sustained sessions with the ole gal, Paul had already learned of certain salient signs that indicated she was about to launch a battery of questions. One of these— namely a heavy swigging at her tumbler—was patently lacking there in the car. But the hunching down of her scrawny neck between her shoulders wasn't. Nor the sudden flutter of hands to and fro from her lap which reminded the young man of his irascible old PoliSci prof at UBC when he was about to launch into one of his daily tirades against Ontario, the "eastern enemy" of B.C.

So Paul was tense, alert, when she leaned in his direction, but still wholly ignorant, of course, of the nature of her interrogation. However, prevarication was second nature to him—as was his ability to clothe such in a flood of quasi-meaningful language. "That's an excellent question, Professor Butterfield," he began. "Excellent because I think it lies at the heart of Jeremy's problem."

"Get on with it," she grunted. "We're not on TV. I don't want flattery for my question. I want a decently considered answer."

That registered with him but he continued smoothly as if she had just praised his eloquence. "He really loves the zoo. And I think when he has served his apprenticeship out he will be certain to secure a good position. Not only that, but to get into managership."

"Apprenticeship?" she said sharply. "Is it a *medieval* establishment?"

He already knew her odd sense of humor. Ventured a smile. "I thought it sounded a bit classier than *trainee* or *low man on the totem pole*. It's just a formality and I happen to know that he's already gained special interest as well as praise." She eased back fractionally and he knew his point was made.

"Just how do you '*happen to know*,' Paul? That seems to me quite important."

This was something he'd been waiting for. "An uncle of mine, my mother's brother, Doctor Wayne Yuen is a veterinarian. He's also on the Board of the Zoo. So is a distant cousin of my father's, Desmond Ip. So you can say I have contacts. But more than that. Jeremy met Desmond on his first day out there. It was he who introduced Jeremy to me."

"I see," she said, playing with her follow-up question and deciding to risk it anyway. "And is Cousin Yip a *family* man? And not another vet, I hope. One doesn't want these boards top heavy with *them*."

Paul eyed her coolly. He suddenly seemed more Chinese as the slant of his eyes was emphasized. Then she rebuked herself for facile racism. "Yes? You were going to say?" She waved a bony finger. Or was it just shaking?

For a second he thought she was suffering some kind of spasm—before realizing she was trying to be encouraging. "No, Dr. Butterfield, Fourth Cousin Yip is as single as Jeremy and I. And he's an architect."

Geraldine relaxed totally. Wittingly or otherwise, her

young Chinese friend had brought her to the subject she most wanted discussed between them.

"I've never heard of a "Gay" zoo," she said. "And I know a lot of zoos as well as having had a lot of gay colleagues."

"Would you like my window up," shouted Debbie from the driver's seat. "As we get further up the valley the wind funnels more strongly."

Geraldine ignored her. Paul said yes. From sitting right behind her, it was blowing much harder into his face. But that was the only respite the presence at his side was prepared to allow him. "Or is it a gay Chinese consortium and how would my Jeremy fit into that?"

Paul carefully launched his response. "I wouldn't call it a *consortium*. Though you might say an Asian *presence*. I think there is a Japanese doctor also on the board. And I wouldn't want to exaggerate the gay factor. Cousin Yip is the only one I know. And Jeremy the only one on staff I've met, either. There could be others, of course. We seem to be everywhere these days." He vouchsafed her an impish grin. "Then I guess they say that about the Chinese, eh?"

This brought her neatly into another part of her agenda. "You haven't mentioned a single woman," she commented. "Then is the place something like Mount Athos in Macedonia where the Eastern Orthodox monks forbid not only women but all female animals on their Aegean peninsula?"

"The place is full of women," he responded, uninterested in monks in Macedonia. "And I'm not just speaking of the domestic staff," he added diplomatically. There are several professionals including an agricultural expert for the farm aspect of the operation. Perhaps that's where you could come in."

She misunderstood him. "I am ignorant of farm husbandry. It is far from my discipline." She wasn't going to be corralled with some cowgirl, she told herself.

"I was thinking more of one scientist to another. More particularly of the privilege it will be for them to have the advice and wisdom of one of your eminence."

Geraldine sat back. The rest of her conversational project could wait. It was nice to sit back in the waft of such praise. She even looked out of the window at the vigorous greenery of ash and alder bordering each side of the broad highway, noted the tall Douglas firs interspersed with waving poplars. She started counting them. Then she stopped and closed veined eyelids. After all that scheming and planning she was now feeling rather tired.

Chapter Nine

Zoo Stories

Fortified by her nap along the freeway— a suspension of consciousness which she was wholly prepared to deny—Geraldine stepped as steadily as she could muster from Deborah's car and surveyed her surroundings. Before her, there in the car park, was the zoo entrance, beyond that the rolling landscape of the animal farm itself, and beyond that, framing the northern horizon, the niveous tips of the North Shore mountains. From whence came, she immediately perceived, not any kind of God's help but a bloody cold wind. In spite it being the month of June she shivered and wished she'd brought a scarf or something.

Debbie saw her tremble and cross her arms. Before the old scientist had time to drop them to her sides, fight back her instincts and declare it a beautiful day, her friend reacted. She took off her leather jacket and then, from under that, a navy blue cardigan and handed that to Geraldine. "Here," she said, "I'm feeling just too hot for both. Would you be a dear and take it for me?"

It was her way of saying sorry for harboring such hostile thoughts about Geraldine during the journey, an all too familiar guilt that had been growing ever since her realization that she'd mistaken her friend's drifting off with a petulant refusal to speak. The guilt was compounded by the fact that with the window rolled up, she had managed to have a few useful words with Paul, first about his window boxes and what he should put in them and then what kind of dog he and Jeremy would have when they'd decided upon when and where they would settle down. All this punctuated, ever so softly, by the faintest of rhythmic snores from the third party.

Geraldine took the cardigan, beamed phonily at her benefactor, said thank you, and then turned her attention once more to the zoo's portal. Although free standing and tall, it was punier than she would have liked. In no way comparable to the elaborate, art nouveau entrance to the Hamburg *Tiergarten* which happened to be the zoo that sprang to mind as she once more fell into the harsh clutches of memory lane. Recalling herself as a girl in her late teens.

She wasn't sure why that was. Maybe the sight of slim Paul gliding towards the ticket office where, he'd told the ladies, as the car had come to a halt, he would call his remote cousin who could in turn alert Jeremy of their arrival.

It was all so vivid. Like her unpleasant dreams when only the dead seemed to surface. But standing there, the cold breeze ruffling her white curls, if now held at bay from her emaciated body, by Debbie's kind gesture of her cardigan, she felt she could smell 1926 and taste with Proustian power the roast chestnuts she had purchased at sixteen or seventeen from the vendor in front of the Tiergarten's wrought iron façade where she had stood with her suddenly taciturn father.

It had been a bleak moment, a sharp and irrevocable turn, taking her finally and brutally out of his perceived image of her as "Daddy's little girl" and leaving him desolate in her adamantine insistence that she was not—never had been—what he had conceived her to be.

Even as a child Geraldine never picked the gentlest language to make her views known. The situation with her Dad at the Hamburg Zoo was a case in point. But their disagreement had really started back in Victoria, British Columbia, the previous year; one evening in the drawing room after dinner when it had surfaced as no more than a mere spat. She had asked him why he wasn't more successful, like Francis Rattenbury, the architect responsible for the B.C. Provincial Parliament Buildings, the Empress Hotel and the Crystal Gardens. Rattenbury had recently cast off his wife and married a much younger woman, an event that had incensed Geraldine.

"I guess all men feel they can discard their first women and take on another at some time in their lives," she'd announced, especially the likes of that beastly Rattenbury. Goodness knows how long he's been slobbering after that slut from Kamloops. Not like you, Dad. You've never exploited your manhood through us poor women, have you? On the other hand, by not being one of the boys, where has it gotten you? No one's ever heard of you as an architect whereas that beastly philanderer has even had the gall to design a courthouse as well as his fancy hotels. And we can guess what goes on in them!"

He hadn't liked that kind of stuff, especially from the lips of a young girl he still saw as a child, and who happened to be his darling daughter. He was wanting to talk about a young foal his partner had bred and which he wished to give his child as a birthday gift .Instead, he was getting this late evening rant when he sought to relax and enjoy a final whisky and soda,

Shocked by both her worldliness and language, he'd turned away—fled upstairs in fact, to complain to Isabella, already in bed, who neither then nor at any other time wished to hear what her daughter had to say. Geraldine's mother was convinced there was something malevolent in that shrill, incessant young voice, something so irreconcilable with her own temperament and upbringing that she turned more and more for consolation to her youngest, her "Benjamin," her beloved son, Stuart.

Further argument had flickered and died some weeks later when Geraldine had refused his gift of the horse. That tension had only dissipated, when, with her future in mind, she reluctantly accepted a maiden voyage to Europe with her parents.

Of course, the opposite of what all of them intended duly happened. Before they'd disembarked from the Mauritania at Southampton, father and daughter were no longer on casual speaking terms, each communicating stagily via mother and wife.

The later contretemps at the Hamburg Zoo had in fact been preceded by a sharp if brief exchange between them at London's Hampton Court—a setting from which a prescient Isabella had removed herself by complaining yet once more of a headache but intent on writing to her Stuart back in British Columbia, and remaining in The Grosvenor Hotel

The next day Father and daughter, perhaps seeking an

armistice, and certainly troubled by these growing rifts between them which now so fissured their very real love, had departed for their trip down the Thames and the magnificent palace Cardinal Wolsey had built for himself in Richmond. But their motives were profoundly at variance in selecting that particular site. Horatio was anxious to visit the subsequent royal palace because it was where the conference authoring his beloved King James version of the Bible had been held. Geraldine's interest was split between the place's association with the powerful Wolsey forced to surrender his grandiose residence to Henry VIII, the wife-slaughtering monarch of two of his five wives, and its famous maze and gardens which had captured her imagination during Miss Eggington's Botany classes at Crofton House.

Father and daughter were crunching across the gravel forecourt towards the Tudor façade in the company of a small group of sightseers as her father was droned on about treading quasi-holy ground (he was referring to the great biblical conference which had brought Christianity so much closer to the heart of the English-speaking world), when Geraldine erupted. She did not speak for long, but loudly enough, distinctly enough, for several heads to turn in her direction. Indeed, it was that which made her falter, even blush—but not before she had savagely informed her father that she thought Christianity a lot of bosh, and its founder a crackpot. She also managed to get out that she would rather he never bring up the subject again with her.

His sole reply was to express sorrow that she felt that way. But in fact, apart from the subsequent rawness duplicated outside the Hamburg Zoo, when he rashly suggested that they were about to see Darwin's idea of human ancestors, neither broached the topic of religion with the other again. Religion remained until death an unhealed sore between them, he questioning where he had failed in his tutelage, she savaged by guilt at her malevolent eloquence and her knowing how to aim it where it would hurt him most.

Why all that long-ago pain should pop up now as they awaited Jeremy was beyond Geraldine. She was quite confident her caustic atheism was not a problem with her two gay young men and that Creationism versus Darwinism or its successors wouldn't likely arise during their walk around the zoo. What was far more likely bothering her was the knowledge that against the backdrop of her indubitable scientific triumphs of discovery lay several messes of human failure which she was only too disposed to gloss over. Her relationship with her Dad...her husband...Pete Eichelbaum, whom she'd ditched...Would it be likewise for her son?

It all suddenly made her feel not only weighted by matters now to remain permanently unresolved, but also a smidge lonely as the only one left from those sanguinary tangos. Instinctively she fell back next to her friend, Deborah—even took her hand, which was immediately there to be clutched.

"Let's get inside, Debbie," she said, clearing her throat. "I think we'll be more out of the wind."

Chapter Ten

Never Too Late

Jeremy stood alone, sweat cooling on his forehead as he rested from shovelling elephant manure, and confronted Nelly, a female baboon with withered dugs and menacing teeth. He would never in a million years have told Geraldine, but as this representative of the genus *Papio* (he'd quickly noted the nomenclature) sat all alone on the slate rock confronting him—unfathomable expressions flowing dimly in her brown eyes—she reminded him of his illustrious grandmother. This was not mere anthropomorphism. Geraldine's eyes were frosty blue and she was the opposite of hirsute. Moreover, those slack teats looked worn and stretched from excessive sucking—and no human being had ever seen his Grandma scratch her bum with such intensity as the elderly baboon now did. But the very isolation of this dog-snouted creature—and Jeremy knew how intensely social was its kind—and those menacing molars, were disturbing reminders of the visitor about to descend upon him. He knew if he were to reach out to stroke that halo of hair he would find it coarse to the touch, just as he also sensed that the old matriarch of her species wouldn't for a moment allow him the privilege of proximity....

But then, he reminded himself sharply, it was a brand new Grandma Geraldine he was about to encounter: one who would no longer wince at his embrace or shift uneasily as she had when he was a child if he reached out for her hair—one from whose now-desiccated lips might actually come comfort rather than the old growl of disapproval of the uncouth young.

These thoughts were interrupted by a somewhat shrill and reedy voice calling his name. Before he turned his blond head he had recognized the owner. Walking towards him were Paul and his cousin, Desmond Ip, who had introduced the two of them. A few paces behind, moving arm in arm and far more slowly, were his grandmother and her friend from the apartment building. As the two Chinese young men and the venerable Anglo-Saxon ladies greeted him with warm smiles, outstretched hands, and in the case of the ladies, proffered cheeks he had the weirdest sense that he was being joined by his family. He grinned inwardly. Why not? After all, they were in a zoo where all sorts of wildly dissimilar beings co-habited—and not just a couple of human subspecies that a Martian probably couldn't distinguish between!

Greetings done, it was Geraldine who spoke up. "Who's your *friend*, Jeremy?"

He was about to say 'I was just about to ask you the same question, Gran,' when he thought better of it. She might be a remake from the awesome and withheld original he'd known as far back as he could remember, but he still wasn't sure of the limits of her recent transformation.

Instead he said simply, "Isn't she a lovely old girl. The

records say she was one of the first animals here at the zoo. She came from San Diego like quite a lot of them did."

"San Diego was very generous at our beginnings," Desmond Ip informed the rest of them. "Hiram Chan who is on their zoo committee knew my father and felt grateful to Vancouver when Dad helped his son to get into Medical School at UBC. Hiram was also responsible for our first bobcat and our first pair of chimps, which they'd bred down there. And if I've got it right, old Nelly came right after that. She arrived with Cassidy and she was already pregnant by old Arthur—so the pack had a good start here."

"All sounds very family, not to say oligarchic" mused Geraldine. Jeremy wasn't sure, though, whether she was referring to the Chinese network or the growing tribe of baboons.

"It was, it was," said Paul, obviously assuming she meant the latter. "The word *zoo* has become such a dirty term nowadays that it's commonplace for zoos to get together and share things. We've benefited from both Portland and Seattle, for example. And recently we've tried to improve our image by becoming donors too."

"We're particularly strong on bald eagles," Cousin Ip amplified. "Human habitat is threatening them down the American west coast and we are happy to replace their national emblem bird so they can release them in more remote areas."

Grandmother Geraldine was already tiring of such zoological knowledge. Besides, it had nothing to do with the motives for her visit, which she was now anxious to implement.

"Desmond," she said, would you be kind enough to

escort my old friend Debbie, here. I would like to walk
between your cousin and my Jeremy as I have something
to say to them of an intimate nature."

At once and in silence—her words forestalled any
kind of flip comment—the group reassembled in the order
she asked. Deborah's silence, however was of a different
order than the others. Apart from slight surprise at her
friend's use of the diminutive when referring to her, she
was rather more pissed off at being delegated to walk with
the one person there who was an utter stranger. Deborah
Tregaskis was essentially a shy person, summoning her
talkative persona only when relaxed with friends like
Geraldine or, earlier, when teaching her high school stu-
dents. But this Chinese gent in a dark three-piece suit and
an obvious familiarity with menagerie practice was a
daunting rarity in her circumscribed world.

Were she not still feeling residual guilt about her
behavior when driving out there, she might well have
demurred in a softly bitchy way. As it was, she merely drew
in breath heavily and accepted his tailored arm when
Desmond Ip drew alongside her. She then reverted to her
natural self and was soon drawing out the young Chinese
architect about his plans to design further buildings in the
expanding zoo complex through which they were walking—and even about his frustrations over what he considered the barbaric taste in domestic architecture of recent
cash-oriented immigrants from Hong Kong and elsewhere
which, he declared roundly, gave younger and integrated
Chinese like himself, a bad name.

Deborah squeezed his arm and said somewhat
ambiguously that for very many people the Taj Mahal was
the most beautiful building in the world. Their conversa-

tion thereupon quickly turned to the threesome walking ahead of them; she wanting to know about Paul, he wishing to know more about Geraldine and her grandson.

The brace of young men in front were at that moment ignoring the rock-littered wolf enclosure they were passing as they listened to the series of questions, often modified by comments of her own, that the old lady had judiciously prepared for them. All her long life Geraldine had gone straight to the heart of things She did so now.

"I have some questions for the both of you and others for you singly. If you don't mind, Paul, I shall start with the subject of Jeremy—not because we're related or any nonsense like that but because I know him best." She paused, as if remembering something. "Well, he is my grandson, of course and knowing what messes all our families have turned out to be, I am most anxious to help. Being gay and free of all that he-man bilge should help him to get off to a good start."

Paul thought that she sounded like an updated *Auntie Mame*. Jeremy wondered where on earth she was going and whether he could bear to listen to it in Paul's company. Paul grinned in anticipation. Jeremy trembled.

"I'm now assuming you both take what you feel for each other seriously. If you don't then for God's sake tell me right away. I would be stupid to waste my time. And goodness knows, I don't exactly have armfuls of that!"

She waited for no answer but forged ahead. "Jeremy tells me that he is happy working here and would like to make the zoo situation his life vocation. And you tell me, Paul, that he can—with a bit of nudge from you towards those relatives—really get somewhere out here in the remote suburbs. In the organization that is—if it proves to be as above board and devoid of commercial motivation as you all seem to claim it is. Now here's where I come in. If it would help by his taking some degree or whatever—diplomas, that kind of thing—I'd be perfectly willing to underwrite such a venture. Even experience at other, let's say more *established*, zoos—if your contacts—and if you don't mind my saying so, they seem to be all over the place—would help him to secure them, I will pay both his travel plus a stipend if he's considered an apprentice and given paltry wages."

Paul murmured "Only San Diego," but the old lady was now firmly in the saddle and impervious to interruption. "But if that means separation, then I'd help you, too, young man. I don't think early separation between a couple is a good thing." She didn't linger over her personal experiences in that quarter but forged ahead. "In fact, it could be perilous and it's my feeling you both need one another. And as a writer, Paul, it doesn't matter too much where you work from at this stage in the game. I will open doors to individuals you'd never dream of for your interview volume. At least they didn't appear in that roster you announced to me back in the apartment. I'd bend the bones of both old colleagues and those who've benefited from my original research as well as Canadians from other disciplines who've crossed my path—enough, if I may be permitted to boast, to make the Canadian *Who's Who* a collection of non-entities. Quite frankly, after such a book appeared, you'd never look back."

"You're too kind," muttered Paul from a near faint, "I could never thank you enough."

Jeremy felt something incumbent as response from him. "And there I was thinking you were just a grandmother when all the time you were a fairy godmother! When I'm not here cleaning out the animals I'll be cleaning your apartment if you want, Grandma!"

"And I'll do all your email answering if you want," added the competitive Paul. "And catalogue your objets d'art and all those photos for free."

The old lady reared back, cackling hoarsely, as if imitating one of the startled zebras they were now passing. "Whoa!" she exclaimed. "What I want from you two is to see you improve yourselves and one another." Then, as she subsided. "And by the way, I want whatever I'm able to do to be a secret" She nodded at Paul. "I don't want your lot thinking they can rely on me," she said. And then turning in the opposite direction. "And what we agree on has nothing to do with that Jesus-infatuated sister or your father either." She paused fractionally before looking straight ahead. "I might tell Deborah, " she added. "She adores knowing everything about everyone—and this way I can please her too."

Chapter Eleven

So Near and Yet So Far

Geraldine let Paul take her to *dim sum*. The persuasion hadn't been easy. She remembered her first *dim sum* with Peter Eichelbaum all those years back on her return to UBC and Vancouver. That hadn't been a pleasant situation. She saw at once that the on-again-off-again situation was wholly over. In a way of course, it had never been much more than a one-night stand. Subsequently she had foolishly allowed him to romanticize that Belgian night—and had acquiesced to his advances on those subsequent occasions in various cities across two continents when it suited her sexual purpose to do so, thus allowing him to perpetuate his pathetic myth of what might some day blossom between them.

When young Paul mentioned *dim sum* the mention of that awkward encounter flowed back and she at once grew restless. She parried the young man's sudden proposal with a string of hastily compiled objections… Chinese lacquer colors hurt her eyes… *dim sum* crowds were too noisy… the washrooms were unhygienic…He laughed at the last and said he would take her to Sun Sui Wah in Richmond where the colors were muted, the patrons quiet and the toilets impeccable. Her concession was not only born of her determination to cling to the vision of the "new Geraldine" that Deborah Tregaskis had sparked. She was equally determined to see that this Paul and her Jeremy were given every chance to do better in relationship than she herself had been able to manage.

Right after the visit to the zoo, buoyed by the experience of addressing the two young men, she had turned to a small volume she'd purchased when she first suspected her grandson's sexual proclivities, but never read. It lived in a small wall closet along with certain precious letters she'd retained, letters mainly from Peter Eichelbaum but also a handful from her father. The book was entitled, *Is There One in Your Family?* and subtitled, *A Comprehensive Guide to Male Homosexual Attitudes, Activities, and Anxieties.* The author was one Algernon Firbank, Ph.D.,Consultant Psychologist at Cedars of Lebanon Hospital, Los Angeles, whose previous books included *Know Your Dog* and *Observing Primates.* It was in the implications of scientific probity in the latter title which had persuaded her to purchase the slim volume from the more dubiously designated Ah Men Press.

Data from this lingered in the crevices of her mind as she and Paul sat themselves down in the Sun Sui Wah at a table, he insisted, where the trolleys bearing *dim sum* would be most frequent and plentiful in number. He was obviously used to ordering for non-Cantonese-speaking patrons, but was most careful, she noted appreciatively, to make quite sure that she understood the dishes on each trolley and which ones she was minded to savor.

In no time several servings of *Har Kow* (shrimp dumplings) and *Sui Mai* (meat dumplings) had collected

on small plates between them. But in spite of his eager
assurances, she only eyed them suspiciously, and decided
they would remain as far as she was concerned. However,
with the arrival of two plates of *Char Sui Pao*, which Paul
described for her as BBQ pork buns and which she found
visually more appealing, she judged it propitious to follow
up on the advice and interrogations offered at her Zoo per-
formance. She sipped her milkless tea, nibbled a portion of
pork bun, and prepared to deliver.

This, however, wasn't quite what Paul had in mind.
First he had some questions of his own to elaborate on her
spate of promises to help his relationship with Jeremy.
More than that, Jeremy himself had also begged his new
lover to get the old lady to spell out in further detail what
she had in mind for her grandson—especially if he were to
risk returning to academe at some point to try to acquire
qualifications beyond his high school diploma. Jeremy
couldn't so facilely dismiss his grandmother as a dotty old
crank. He was still trying to grapple with her abrupt ability at ninety-six to modify her ways in certain respects.

Geraldine listened with unaccustomed patience and
quickly answered all that was asked of her. She was used to
the dollar and cents materialism of the young and in any
case, had spent a lifetime dealing with data and making
pertinent decisions.

As she was tucking hungrily into a fried prawn she
suddenly looked up over the small pyramid of the crus-
taceans and asked Paul how far he was prepared to go in
sustaining and encouraging her grandson should Jeremy
falter or become excessively defeatist. "I tell you quite
frankly, young Paul, it is my greatest fear for him since I
learned he'd fled back to his father when his relationship

with his previous partner had come apart."

Paul was all reassurance, and not for the first time Geraldine told herself that he was far more mature than his looks suggested. She warmed yet more to him and told herself that at the earliest possible moment she would remind Jeremy of how lucky he was to have met him, and to work harder than he'd ever done in his short life at being a proper companion to this jet-eyed, quick-spoken lad from whom ideas and observations tumbled with the prodigality of a waterfall.

"Jeremy has been hurt, Dr. Butterfield. Many people have contributed, I think. It will take not only a lot of effort from us but time, too, to get him to trust anybody."

Geraldine came quickly to a decision she had pondered but postponed up to that point. "You can call me Grandma if you like." She sounded almost shy.

Paul stopped munching and lowered his chopsticks. Her words were music. They filled him with daring. "Can—can I call you Gran? Like Jeremy does behind your back?"

Geraldine did likewise with her fork. She considered her plate with the litter of shrimp tails on its circumference. "I don't see why not," she said, not looking at him. "At least when its just the two of us or with Jeremy along." Then she did eye him. "Of course, when we're with strangers—say when we're working on our book—then it should be Dr. Butterfield, I think."

"Of course," he replied. "I was only thinking of when we were 'family.'"

"Funny," she said. "The way one uses the word 'family' nowadays." But what she was really thinking was how this young man's words made her keen to have a family—

one comprising just the three of them. Such notions were completely new to her, Previously she'd thought of family as a weighty obstacle to fulfillment of her blazing ambition. The young man sitting opposite was probably animated with a similar driving hunger to succeed. She grabbed a portion of egg roll with her fingers(it had failed to prove susceptible to her fork).

Buoyed by that assumption she decided to press deeper. "And you, Paul. Am I right in thinking that you'll go whole hog after your goals? That you're determined to be a success in your writing—come hell or high water?"

With his chopsticks Paul deftly lifted a piece of fried squid from the saucer nearest to him. She seemed obsessed with the business of ambition. Even so, he saw no reason to deny her. "I certainly want to be at the top of my field." (*barest pause*) "Grandma. I've always wanted to be up front—just ask my Mom and Dad. Paul D. Wong isn't interested in being second best in *anything*."

He gave her his special smile—the mischievous one accompanied by a coy flicker of his long eyelashes. "And that goes for my partner too. I want Jeremy not just to be a topnotch zoo man but the *best* there is. We're going to breathe the same sweet air up there in the good ole land of success."

Geraldine shoveled an obstinate grain of rice with her upturned fork. "I'm sure you want the best for you both. I saw that in you, Paul, right from the start. I just want to make sure that he doesn't get hurt as you fight your own way to the top. You see, young man, he simply doesn't have the ambition you have. Just like his father. Never will. So you must have enough, not just for the two of you, but help him go forward by being very gentle and imaginative, to try to see what it's like to be in his shoes."

"Wearing his moccasins?" said Paul, winningly.

Geraldine bestowed on him her most expansive smile. "*Exactly,*" she said. "I see we're on the same wavelength, and that makes me very happy."

In the coziest of moods they both ate more *dim sum* dishes than they had anticipated and departed the Sun Sui Wah mildly overstuffed and with Paul feeling that major hurdles in his future life had been successfully surmounted, while Geraldine, declining the restaurant facilities, had laid her mental agenda wholly to rest. She was now concentrating on a sustained visit to those intimate appliances awaiting her in the privacy of her own bathroom. A familiar goal…

Chapter Twelve

All Kinds of Blindness

For a time it looked as if Geraldine was back to what she—but no one else—had come to regard as normal. She rarely if ever sortied from her apartment and was again vigilant in the scrutiny of all would-be visitors. That dratted bathroom was a constant and with the slight modification of a brand name as she toyed alternatively with Ballantines and Johnny Walker (Black Label), her alcoholic input remained the same.

True, as a result of a further nudge from Deborah Tregaskis, who caught her in the act of writing a letter to her son, Hugh, she was persuaded to sign herself off with a "Your loving Mother" rather than the "Your Biological Mother, Geraldine Butterfield." But that was the end of any contribution to new approaches from her friend.

In fact the only other variant in the growing weeks that had now accumulated since the successive but still individual visits from Jeremy (whose work at the zoo made his trips to her infrequent) and those of Paul (whose interviews with her became routine), was a certain shift in emphasis. The subtle reasons behind this change were not at first apparent to either of them. It wasn't until Paul had begun his more specific and carefully crafted questions about her early discoveries in the lab, and his ever so delicate dipping into the nature of her personal life at that time that he realized he already had far more of Geraldine on tape than he could possibly use without throwing his lofty Canadian *Pantheon* hopelessly out of balance.

He woke one night in the feverish clutch of Jeremy's arms at the latter's zoo employee's cabin when his lover quickly asked if anything was the matter. He sleepily replied, "Oh God, I think there might have to be two, not just one!" Jeremy thought he was referring to lovers and lay awake until dawn, when he again anxiously roused Paul who made it mercifully clear that books, not bodies, had been the substance of his nightmare.

During roughly the same period, Geraldine realized that, far from being a chore, or worse, a potential embarrassment, letting a young man into her past life via the deft tools of his words was not that unpleasant. Indeed, it started to give shape to what had hitherto been a lifelong series of isolated incidents—however dramatic each had been. Now she began to perceive a contour that connected the accomplished scientist to the precocious child: the restless and rebellious girl who stirred whenever she turned her attention from the rigid rationality of her laboratory space to the murk and ill-defined attitudes of a world where unlettered and undisciplined egos roamed and reigned. True, she saw her mistakes, but the ever-so-diplomatic Paul showed her how to forgive herself and—though still very tentatively-how she might also forgive others. It was then that she deliberately if covertly embarked upon a campaign to persuade her delectable Chinese scribe that she was surely worthy of a book devoted solely to herself.

Paul had already come to this conclusion and, as a result of his nocturnal utterance and subsequent clarification before sex and breakfast, secured Jeremy's enthusiastic endorsement of what would be tantamount to his prickly grandmother's biography. Thus the very next session between "Granny Geraldine" (as Paul now secretly entitled her), and "my Chinese pal, Paul" (as she invariably described him to Deborah), took on a quite different flavor from any of its predecessors.

Things began cozily enough. The subject of her burgeoning career seemed both innocuous and attractive in his interpretation, until they reached a signal event in her early life as a blossoming research chemist of which she was not only less than proud but most reluctant to revisit.

The time was April, 1939, when the increasingly distinguished but still young professor (now 33), who was deeply involved in brain research into abnormal chromosomes present in patients with the context of Down's syndrome, received an invitation to speak to the Medical Faculty of the University of Luxembourg. The previous summer she had heard that a group of researchers had gathered in Echternach, Luxembourg, and that a couple of papers they'd read suggested some exciting research germane to her field.

She had accepted the Luxembourg invitation but not primarily for professional reasons. Like many in that post-Munich period, she saw the gathering of Teutonic shadows over Europe and was prompted to pay a last-minute visit to the Continent before returning to her post at Yale and The Giselle Institute where she was a Visiting Fellow. With her keen knowledge of Europe. She was well aware that both the capital city of the tiny country of Luxembourg and the town of Echternach were but a stone's throw from Vianden on the edge of the Ardennes Forest.

Vianden was an almost mystical place for her. It was where her schoolgirl hero, Victor Hugo, spent one of his latter exiles. If, as in all likelihood, the second major war in the twentieth century was about to occur, then she herself, once back in North America and cut off from both England and Europe, would feel something of an exile from so many places she knew and loved. It was not a prospect she had relished.

Her apprehension was allayed soon after her arrival in the Grand Duchy. On her second day in the University's Medical Faculty, she was introduced to a blonde, brown-eyed young woman who was about ten years her junior and who immediately took her fancy as fluently English-speaking, frank and friendly. She turned out to be working in the same field and making astonishingly similar discoveries. By the third day, when Ilse had shown Geraldine her lab, her notes, and explained that an infant brother with Down's syndrome back home in Vienna had sparked her career, the Canadian was becoming positively fond of this figure in lab-coat over a fashionable skirt who spoke English with such a charming Austrian accent.

Adolf Hitler and his Anschlüss, *Fräulein Doktor Rosen* explained, was the reason for her current sojourn in Luxembourg. She was Jewish and her father, a tailor with premises tucked away in the narrow huddle of shops below St. Stephen's Cathedral, had insisted she take the research position even though it was only for one year. That was sufficient time, an insouciant Herr Rosen was sure, for the Fuehrer to be satisfied with German territorial claims in

Europe, and to gracefully retire to his Bavarian home in Bertchesgarten. Ilse would then return to Vienna, she enthusiastically explained to the distinguished Canadian scientist and write up her findings, which she was convinced would result in a giant leap forward in the treatment of Down's syndrome.

Geraldine was genuinely excited by Ilse's research. And she found it enormously encouraging that far away in Vienna a young woman was experiencing the same frustrations, the same break-throughs that she had been experiencing on the other side of the Atlantic. Moreover, the fiercely anti-religious Geraldine savoured the fact that Ilse's significant research was being trumpeted in small and backward Echternach, known to the world primarily for its medieval festival of Christian flummery, the *Feast of the Precious Blood.*

Geraldine was about to inflict on Paul a refreshing diatribe on obsolete religious rituals when her would-be interrogator changed his tack. He was hardly allowing her to get up steam on any darned subject before interrupting with some quick, stabbing question that put her right off track. It was thus when she was delivering on Ilse.

"And did you feel something special for Dr Rosen?"

"I've already told you. Here was a young woman from halfway round the world working in my field. Or close to my field. How many times do I have to say?"

"That's not what I'm asking, Grandma Geraldine. I got all that down. Now I want the human stuff. The stuff that makes you a real person and not just ambition in a white coat."

She managed to hold back her retort. Waited for him to go on.

"You said she was attractive. You told me and Jeremy way back about those girls at Crofton House. Did you think of anything like that with Ilse? Were you sexually attracted to her? Even if nothing happened, was there anything like that between you? Maybe from her side?"

For a moment Geraldine felt triumph. "Certainly not! You'd better get this clear right now as you obviously didn't in that earlier session. There isn't a Sapphic bone in my body. The idea makes me want to puke!" She paused, thinking quickly. "Mind you, I've nothing against that kind of thing for others. My colleague, Professor Ethel Dilsworth at McGill was a case in point. Brilliant woman—should've got a Nobel for her work on uterine cancer if the whole world hadn't known she was living with that dumb Betty Newcombe, the Olympic swimmer."

Paul wasn't to be deterred. "Even so, you brought up Ilse Rosen. We can't just hang her out there to dry. Or was it just the conference that you wanted to talk about? *Please* co-operate, *Grandmamma*", (in his anxiety he offered her a new title). "But if there's something else, then somehow we should get it in. The reader will be much more attentive than with just bare bones stuff. And you'll come out of it looking better, I promise. After all, Frau Grandma Doktor, it was all so many years ago you can hardly hurt anybody by now."

"I had no intention of doing so, Paul. But there are things…Well, things that, even after all this time, are difficult to get off one's chest. After all, one was so much younger, history had so much horror still to reveal. And looking back, we were all guilty, all of us to blame. Not just Nazis. Germans…"

But Paul was hardly listening to her. Her tone had

changed. He knew she was about to open up something that festered deep, deep inside. He sat back, ballpoint poised (she had said after the first three sessions that the sight of his laptop impeded her thought processes). He only had to wait…

"By the weekend Ilse and I had covered an enormous field. There was nothing more for her to show me and I could already see that her Down's research could very well lead to my primary interest which was amaurosis in children—particularly any cerebral links."

"Whoa!" interrupted Paul. "What the hell is amaurosis?"

Geraldine put on her kindly teacher's look. "It was a fashionable term at the time. Dates from the mid 17th century and comes from the Greek for *dim*. Can I continue?

Paul nodded, returning a smile as broad as hers.

"Most of my colleagues at the time were satisfied with some kind of cerebral link to the optic nerve. But not Ilse! She wasn't for a moment fooled by the lack of any visible change in the eye itself. Then, of course, she was really pursuing Down's syndrome and not blindness at all. At any rate, I asked her if she'd ever visited nearby Vianden which I only knew then from the guide books but got to know much better on a later visit."(Geraldine was careful to make no mention of Peter Eichelbaum as being her companion on the subsequent trip—knowing all too well how Paul would have pursued that like a famished ferret.)

"She replied that she hadn't and had always wanted to see the Forest of the Ardennes and find out how it compared with her native Wienerwald. At first our time there was quite idyllic. We found an exquisite little restaurant that served a delicious wild boar specialty. And the spring growth in the woods was so soothing to urban eyes like ours. Then—then I was happy to show her where Victor Hugo stayed in exile. But in retrospect that was a mistake. Her mood changed when she had digested the historic facts. Oh, in many ways, she remained her ebullient self but it was then, for the first time, she brought up the possibility of her changing her academic venue. To be quite honest, she went further than that. Asked me what the possibilities were for her to join me at Yale. I told her of course, that I was merely a Visiting Fellow there and had absolutely no say in such matters. That I wasn't even an American citizen and all that kind of stuff.

"But she absolutely refused to give up. She persisted—pleaded if you like. Over and over again I had to repeat that my own field of research was so totally restricted, that in fact I faced so much skepticism and opposition—ah, those bloody men!—that there was no place for two of us—let alone for two women. Besides, there were simply no financial resources for such a project. I told her that there was nothing more to say, but she simply wouldn't take no for an answer—even when I began to get, well, kind of cross. She still pressured me—changing her tack, though. She suggested that Austria was no longer safe for a Jew like her."

Geraldine licked dry lips. Paul was only too aware how difficult she was finding these memories. He just looked at her impassively, afraid to utter a single word, less it distract her. But the old woman had the bit between her teeth. She couldn't have stopped, even if she'd wanted to.

"I—I had to confess that I was by nature a loner. That I'd never worked in a team, even when that would have been to my advantage. My research at that time was really only suitable for a single-handed approach and that her own work was surely along similar lines. But all I got was hysterical argument. Not really an argument but a pleading to help her get out of her country. She said that she'd planned to ask me, even before I arrived in Luxembourg."

Geraldine took in a breath so violent that it made her wheeze. "She never did give up. She phoned me twice in London before I went home. And then back in New Haven I got letters. Right into that fall and after Hitler's invasion of Poland.

"Of course, none of us had any idea of what lay in store for the likes of Ilse and her people. Maybe we didn't want to think of what might happen. After that fall of 1939 I never heard from Doctor Rosen again. But I know now I shirked my responsibility. Not as a scientist, not even as a woman, but as a human being. Why was I was so negative over her suggestion right off the bat? Because deep down I was jealous of her—jealous of her brilliance and her success at such an early age. But even more, I was jealous for my own reputation.

"I tell you Paul, since 1945 when I saw those pictures in a British newspaper...the camps...the corpses... my guilt has never gone away. I can never just say let's blame the Germans or the Austrians, or let's blame the anti-Semites who are still everywhere. The truth is we are *all* to blame for what we *didn't* do. So, young Paul, I shall go to my grave with that guilt still on my conscience. You'd better get all that down. It won't change anything. That girl's pleas still inhabit my ears. But I'd be ashamed of even more if I were to still skirt the truth of Ilse Rosen and my personal contribution to her fate."

Paul reached over to hold her trembling hand—mistaking age for the rigors of confession, but she quickly withdrew it. His voice surprised him in its register when he spoke; now so gruff, so hoarse. "Thanks for telling me all that. I'll go now Grandma, go and work on what you've just said. I'll bring it back tomorrow so you can check it."

Geraldine smiled. "I don't think there'll be need of much editing." She got to her feet with a slight wobble. "I don't know about you, Paul, but I really could do with another Scotch."

Even if he'd been an ardent teetotaler he would have gladly downed another glass of the foul-tasting stuff out of identification with her at that special moment between them.

Chapter Thirteen

The Spur of Memory

"So here we are again," said Geraldine, settling herself on her balcony in response to the better change in the weather and welcoming Paul to her favorite *Bleu d'Auvergne* cheese and equally un-appreciated hard crackers that unpleasantly pressed her dentures against sometimes sore gums. She then encouraged his visit to the fridge for her own liquid requirements. He poured her a *Laphraoig* from a bottle he had brought her as a gift but himself reverted to a fizzy tumbler of *Pellegrini* water—a substance which he had been about to also mix with her Single Malt until she had screamed 'blasphemy!' at his back, causing him almost to drop both mineral water *and* whisky. Her composure was fully recovered—as was his—by the time he'd brought her an unalloyed beverage and she announced that she was now ready and willing to provide him with further cameos from her life.

She had a couple of requests, however. Paul waited patiently. Geraldine's asides were often lengthy—attempts to divert or shorten them, perilous.

"For reasons that will be apparent, I would prefer to

leave the details of my meeting my future husband and our marriage to later. And that also goes for the birth of my son, Hugh. The grandchildren will obviously come after that."

Geraldine eased herself tenderly on the tubular lounge chair. That morning more bones ached in diverse parts of her body than usual—though for the usual unspecified reasons.

"I should also like to make this session shorter than the last one. I felt quite drained after it and suffered a virtually sleepless night."

Paul still refrained from opening his mouth. He had quickly learned that when she waved her tumbler gently to and fro it wasn't simply due to a shaky hand but was an infallible sign she was in thinking high gear and preparing to utter.

"I would like today to discuss my wartime experiences at McGill and my contacts with several of those connected with the Manhattan project—especially in the Canadian context of Chalk River. I met most of the famous spies, you see, Alfred Nunn May, Klaus Fuchs and Pontecorvo? That crowd? Through a young lab technician I befriended. Would that interest you?"

Paul knew it was now his turn.

"Sounds fascinating, Grandmama Butterfield."

Geraldine was ever all ears for terms of address—addressing *her*, that is. "Skip the Butterfield. Remember our agreement?"

Paul bowed his sleek black head to just a slight deferential degree—the right side of obsequiousness. She nodded. Satisfied.

"I know absolutely nothing about that lot—except

that they were a bunch of spies. Do, please go on."

She did. But in her own fashion. "Misguided idealists was what they were. Idiots and ostriches rather than crooks. Anyway, I didn't know them all that well. It was Jack Wesley that I knew best—and he turned out every bit as interesting as the whole bunch of `em. He was the first homosexual I really got to know. You and Jeremy have a lot to thank him for, come to think of it.

Paul stiffened but remained silent. Whether the old girl liked it or not, he wasn't going to turn this book of her recollections into some kind of gay saga—just because she was happy about his relationship with her grandson. Jeremy's new lover was ambitious. Not for Paul Wong some hole-in-the corner gay publishing press that only served a marginalized minority!

Poor Paul. He knew he was smart enough. Wasn't he rapidly assimilating the import of the numerous highlights of Geraldine's long and distinguished career? Yet the the tortuous and often devious links between those highlights, the links that made sense of her life, continued to elude him.

"It had nothing to do with Jack's sexual problems, incidentally, but a whole lot of other baggage the poor man carried. I now see so much of him in Jeremy. The defeatist element for one thing. When he went back to Winnipeg after the war and failed his degree, his bullying father told him he would be a failure for the rest of his life. Jack acted exactly the way my son, Hugh, acted. He never did escape the scar, even though he was doing pretty well by the second time I met him—by which time he'd become a junior executive with a major pharmaceutical company that was courting me. Mind you, he still had a lot of phony aggression. A sort of fake 'superman' attitude? That alone took me ages to persuade him to drop—which he only did when he finally saw I was no threat. Not to his career, mind. I'd finally convinced him that I wasn't a snob and didn't despise him as a commercial traveler."

With difficulty, Paul suppressed a snigger. He was really beginning to like as well as admire this cantankerous old bird—but that didn't mean he had to throw his brains out the window. (Or in this case, over the balcony.)

"Naturally I wore myself out showing that I couldn't care less what degrees he'd earned—as long as he knew what he was talking about when representing his firm. Earlier, when I first met the prickly boy in my lab at Chalk River where he'd come to work, he was so full of resentment and suspicion that he assumed I was his mortal enemy. Probably the result of some bitch school teacher who picked on him or made a pass at him. He was cute, as I've said. In any event, I knew I had to get that gay business out in the open and let him know where I stood on that if we were to get anywhere."

"Right from the start, you see, I sensed he was a queer." She darted Paul a glance, could read nothing there. Continued. "In those days, you have to realize young man, that being gay, as we say so freely nowadays, wasn't quite as respectable as it has subsequently become."

Paul was glad he hadn't risen to the bait of "queer"— in fact was even more determined to hear her out over this closety guy she'd known, so long as she got quickly onto her spies and whatever her connection with *them* was. He was even hoping that maybe she'd come up with something juicy like her lab boy friend blowing a visiting J. Robert Oppenheimer, or whatever. A little sexual hanky-panky would do no harm to the sales of a biography of a nonagenarian woman biochemist with a penchant for zoos—especially in his discreet hands. Not though, for one moment, did he lose sight of the risk of portraying her in too sour a light and thus jeopardizing her generous attitudes towards himself and his cherished Jeremy.

Geraldine did something again in Paul's company that she rarely did in Deborah's. She held up her empty glass and smiled sweetly. "I am about to traverse difficult waters," she announced, " but I shall need more than water in there to cross them successfully."

By the time he returned she was ready to proceed. " I have mentioned how my grandson appears to share Jack's defeatism—or did so until you came along and provided him with hope and courage." Geraldine smiled at Paul so expansively that she had suddenly to straighten her face, knowing that her upper denture's position was at best precarious. Satisfied that her goodwill was palpable, she stroked one of the wayward hairs that sprouted askew from her chin with her free hand and continued. "But there is one person whom I haven't mentioned at all that bore a striking physical resemblance to young Jack, and that is my late brother, Stuart. He and Jack both wore the trappings of golden youth—tall, blue-eyed, fair hair—all that nonsense. Only there the similarities ended. Sharply. For whereas Jack was the pariah of his horrible family, always treated by that bastard father as a disaster and, I suspect, ignored by his vacuous and narcissistic mother, my own brother Stuart was the apple of Mother's eye and regarded by my doting father as owning to the intelligence and aptitude that, in all modesty, I have to say were exclusively his daughter's.

"A premature death in a skiing accident on Mt. Baker insured that he was enshrined securely in their memories as the beloved son who would have inherited the earth had he lived and there was nothing I could do, nothing indeed that I *accomplished*, that could subtract from their exclusive worship at his shrine."

She shifted her weight. "Well, enough of that. I mention it only to provide a reason for my initial interest in a lab assistant who was to eventually blossom into a sales rep for a major pharmaceutical firm but who would still remain convinced that at bottom he was zilch—nothing. In short, Paul, I want you to understand that I wasn't at that period in my career, or later, for that matter, the slightest bit interested in "broken reeds." I had a couple of women colleagues who were—so while they fluttered and squawked like anxious hens over those younger men and women who came into their range of interest in lab or classroom, I instead stayed faithful to my true vocation, which had was nothing to do with any of the string of clichés about womanhood. Not surprisingly, I soon surpassed both Dr. Louise Gifford and Dr. Helen Gonzales in my work, and my discoveries I'm proud to say, have benefited more than just one screwed-up youth here and another softy mother's boy there. In short I stayed loyal to my professional research and never for one moment have I regretted it!"

Her gnarled hand shook as it transported her glass to her mouth. "Now make sure you get this down, Paul. Make sure that thing's switched on!

"That isolation I embraced, which separated me from other women in the profession, has been worth more than all the female nonsense that men have dreamed up for us over the centuries. And later on in these interviews I'll recite chapter and verse the skullduggery my attitude enabled me to miss, such as that unhappy Rosalind Franklin and her treatment by those bastards over DNA."

She slowed her pace, not so much for dramatic effect but because she had to swallow a cumbersome degree of spittle that had irritatingly accumulated with her oration. Geraldine also took the occasion to wonder, fleetingly, whether her declaration was too strong for those young ears across the aisle separating them—delicately sculpted Chinese ears which she was sure were unused to such a blunt *credo* from the mouth of a woman.

She then decided that, whatever Paul wanted her to say, she wasn't going to soft-pedal her lifelong quest to reach that plateau where hitherto only men walked, leaving the women to pick up the wounded relics of the male rat-race and smother them with 'motherly' comfort. In fact, everything Geraldine hated about conventional relations between the sexes was summed up in such sterile panaceas as '*Come to Mummy and she'll kiss it better*' or the belief that breasts were designed only for suckling infants, or for some hapless male to snuggle up between.

When she picked up the threads of her story again it was with a renewed vigor—fuelled by the familiar surge of anger at the thought of such images. "However, there remains Jack. Right up to the end, though, when we were alone he'd call himself a peddler rather than a sales rep! In some ways he was more English than Canadian. And certainly he seemed rather odd in our research world with that relentless sense of class of his. But there was also his extreme sensitivity about his lack of credentials—academic or scientific."

Paul nudged her gently. "Jack was that important to you, Grandmama? There must have been something special about him. After all, you were up to your ears in your work. As a laboratory assistant—well, he must've been on another plane."

She eyed him for a moment. His pulse became more regular when he could see nothing baleful in her expression. He relaxed further, smiled with relief when her next words told him he had hit pay dirt.

"That's quite perceptive. There was indeed something very special about Master Jack Wesley, that transcended all the other stuff. He was *bright*, you see. He could follow what I was saying, picked up things right away. And I'm a woman who both then and now can't stand those who're dull and slow—however sweet and virtuous they might be.

"When I have conversation I want the talk to be fifty-fifty. Like tennis. I want the ball lobbed right back. That's why, right after we met, Paul, I knew you and I would get on. Nothing's more depressing than to say something and meet a blank stare in response. Well, no fear of that with our Jack—even though he could be a bugger with his snide remarks."

Paul thought it time he'd said something—*à propos* or not. "*Reparteé*, Grandmother, that's what we both like, isn't it?"

Her white hair bobbed and he had to take that as her assent. Her words were elsewhere. "Funny that I should mention tennis—because that's what led from Jack to his spy friends. They taught him to play, you see. It was all to do with their pretending to treat him as an equal. They didn't play tennis with anyone else there. Of course, they could have been trying to recruit him—probably were. But

like so many bright types, especially the Brits, I have to
keep saying, when the class business was involved—either
being praised or sneered at—they turn to putty, put their
intelligence on hold."

"Flattery will get you somewhere," Paul murmured,
speaking from experience.

But again she ignored him. "When he invited me to
meet them—and were they ever itching to do so when he
told them I was a research scientist at McGill. I even went
to Chalk River and stood there at the net as he played with
that slippery Alan Nunn-May.

"I could see what was going on. I was well placed, you
see, Paul—as a female scientist up against the male hege-
mony—to understand what they were up to with Jack.
They were *patronizing* him. You always read about people
getting hot under the collar for being patronized, but that's
misleading. Most people enjoy it until they twig. My male
colleagues, though, and this goes right back to my stint at
Columbia before Oxford, and back again on this side of the
Atlantic at Yale, were all so bloody crude that I saw
through 'em from the word go.

"Maybe those three at Chalk River weren't crude
exactly, perhaps their spy training had taught them a
smidgeon of subtlety. But they certainly larded the praise
on old Jack. Even when he failed to win his serve, Nunn-
May was applauding him and the other two standing with
me were clapping when he'd just lost a game at love. But it
wasn't all quite one-way I was to learn. They refused to
believe he was just a lab boy—even when he kept telling
them he was. They couldn't get over the fact he was so
darned smart—smart-ass too, to tell the truth—and until
it was all over and they'd left, I'm pretty sure they thought

he was incognito on some special assignment.

"That's one thing about spies. They think everyone else is too! Even a seventeen-year-old kid. Of course, we didn't know they were spies then. No one did. But I tell you, by just meeting them in Jack's company, and fending off their questions, I thought them a peculiar bunch. Jack didn't of course. We had a couple of almighty rows about that. They were his heroes, you see. But, whenever I said anything negative, he thought I was hinting they had the hots for him and went into hysterics—or his equivalent, which meant the pouts. And that was even after he'd fessed up to me about being gay. Then it was always back to that. We'd be chatting about Pontecorvo's poor backhand or how poor a physicist Klaus Fuchs was and he'd rant and rave about how decent they both were and that I was maybe jealous!"

A worm turned in Paul. "And were you?" he snapped.

Shriveled Geraldine, although horizontal, suddenly grew longer. " I see I've exhausted your interest in Chalk River, young man. I should have stayed with McGill and my first major break-through." Her words were even, but the tone icy.

Paul made no answer. He was too busy cursing himself for momentarily losing his cool. She wasn't through, though. "I had all to say that I wish to about jealousy yesterday. I'll trouble you not to raise the subject again. I've been honest with you—and if you intend to be likewise with me then I suggest you ask me about the Butterfield-Fletcher Findings. And if my role in that troubles you, you might want to go onto my later work in the field when I was asked to head the team at UCLA."

He was already nodding vigorously in agreement but

she was no longer minded to be conciliatory, let alone co-operative in any respect. "But that must await our next session as I have several idiots to telephone and musn't lose any more energy over this interview business."

Paul could see that the "new Geraldine" was no longer present. Moreover, he wasn't sure—given that—how much longer "the super patient Paul" could last. He got wearily to his feet. "I can see myself out, Grandmama," he said wearily. "I'll be in touch."

He didn't hear her murmur in his wake: "You sound just like Deborah, when you're in a snit."

She waited until she heard the front door close before draining her drink and picking up the phone to take her grumpiness out on her friend in the apartment below her.

Chapter Fourteen

He Who Would Valiant Be

Hugh was not alone when he next visited his mother. His daughter, Rebecca, accompanied him. It was the only way she would have seen the girl, Geraldine later told Deborah. At first the old lady ignored her granddaughter who sat stiff and silent on an upholstered high back chair in the crowded living room, her hands on her lap, her eyes downcast. Pretending, her grandmother thought, to be modest.

Geraldine sat so that she could ignore the figure of offending piety and confronted her son, who was sitting as close as he could get to the balcony window (it was pouring rain) as he fired carefully framed questions at her concerning her health.

Hugh did not tell her, but he had the day before received another phone call from Dr. Robert Caskie about his aged mother. There'd been the usual complaints about her lack of co-operation. She'd spoken briefly to her physician of her arthritis, her wild cycle between constipation and diarrhea, her "malfunctioning taste-buds"(her own term), her sore eyes and wobbly legs. But all attempts by the doctor to get her to undergo some bloodwork at his adjacent lab and possible X-rays were flatly refused. "Whatever is wrong internally, Caskie," she told him, "must stay so. I want no more indignities of that nature and at my age, all cellular growth is sufficiently slowed for nothing to happen in too much of a hurry. So—if you'll forgive the irony—that's something I can live with. What I want from you is some medication that will quicken my responses. I am so damned frustrated by all this slowing down. If you are conversant with the metaphors of natural history—I currently have the disposition of a fox harnessed to the body of a sloth. And it is driving me mad!"

He was conversant enough with these complaints and her concomitant obduracy to know that both threats and coaxing were lost on her. As usual, all efforts exhausted, he called her son. "I'm sure you'll understand, Dr. Woodbridge, if she persists in these refusals to undergo examination—if she should suffer cardiac arrest, which seems highly likely—it will put me in the most awkward light. I speak professionally. She is technically my patient but there is a total failure to collaborate. If you'll forgive me saying so, if she were not your son, Dr. Woodbridge, I would have long been shot of her."

Hugh once more had to swallow hard, suppress the words of dutiful defense over his mother's bloody intransigence, even as they formed. "Of course I understand, Doctor. This isn't the first time, is it? We—we both will have our records. My mother would not want to cause you professional injury—let alone create a scandal. I am sure she is as anxious as I am to see that at her demise and the accompanying publicity for one of her eminence, you get due credit for keeping her in reasonable health and spirits to such a very advanced age. Then I'm sure you already know how grateful we the family are, for your care and guidance over recent years."

He stopped right there. Afraid he'd be sick if the old fart persisted and he had to pour out more sickly emollients on his mother's behalf. In any case, she allowed him no more time for reflection along those lines. She was now complaining of her irregularities and chafing restrictions of her body to her son. It was as if she made no distinction between the plump little Scot and himself. He closed his eyes. It was all so *déjà vu*. Then he stirred and divested himself of the sentiments which he knew would either end with her angrily showing them the door or in a state of tearful vulnerability that she would take months to forgive.

"I've told you a hundred times before, Mother, it is quite impossible for me to act as your doctor. It would be demanding just too much of your flesh and blood. I don't have—never have had—the objectivity you seem to bring to everything. You must forgive me. I just can't do it."

To his surprise, her response was different from what it had ever been in the past.

"I understand, Son. I've met very few people, as a matter of fact, who are prepared to look facts in the face. Something I've been doing it for a very long time. That's what science is all about. And then there's the other thing. When you get to my age, it's either talk or silence—perpetual. Wake or sleep—everlasting. I don't have the minutes left to pussyfoot around and think up bland little euphemisms. I guess that's why I've hurt certain folk's feelings. I call a spade a spade because there isn't much time left to call it anything at all."

She could see that neither father nor daughter liked

this kind of talk. He just shifted his feet and stared out at the Burrard Street bridge as if it had just been erected. Rebecca gazed heavenward as if life's consolations were inscribed somewhere up there on the ceiling. But Geraldine wasn't quite ready to give up. They'd come there of their own volition so they'd have to pay the price of hearing an old woman out. "I've been taking a little advice from my friend, Deborah. Just a smidgeon, mind you. She offers so much you'd drown if you took it all! Anyway, I want us all to get on a little better than we have in the past."

"Praise the Lord!" exclaimed her granddaughter.

"No! I thought I said it was *Debbie* who was responsible! In any case, child, don't interrupt." When it came to that religious claptrap Geraldine wasn't about to make any concessions.

"I now have a quite nice relationship with Jeremy and his new friend, Paul."

Another hiss from Rebecca. Geraldine glanced sharply at her but decided that she would put up with such noises—so long as J.C. and his celestial relatives weren't invoked.

"Who's Paul?" her son asked. " I hope he's not another disaster like that previous William."

"He's collaborating with me over a fascinating book about my career. He's also got Jeremy an interesting job out at the Greater Vancouver Zoo. As a matter of fact they're quite splendid for one another." She deliberately paused before her next item of information. "He was born in Victoria and is a UBC graduate—of Chinese ancestry," she added.

She watched both of them jerk but neither spoke. Her reference to her change of heart was far too recent for either of them to abandon their caution with her.

She went on: "He's an excellent questioner—though he prefers the word *interlocutor*. He fully understands the need for, shall we say, a certain haste—given the lengthy territory we have to cover."

"Haste?" queried Hugh.

"Speed, expedition—take your pick. But he knows perfectly well that, at going on ninety-seven, I could depart at any moment. The Chinese, Hugh, have a proper sense of respect for their elderly—take darn good care of `em—but they're also realists."

She didn't add that she was perfectly aware that Paul's realism extended to the limited time she might have left to implement the financial plans she'd outlined for him and Jeremy. But then Hugh, she knew, had his own agenda relating to how much time she had left. So instead she said: "You might consider a Chinese spouse, yourself. She'd likely be a happy balance for your own deficiencies. I've observed something along those lines with Paul and Jeremy. I could ask Paul…"

Her son twiddled his thumbs, suddenly brimful of sympathy for her physician. "There's absolutely no comparison, Mother. I can see nothing whatever in common between us."

He didn't elaborate on whether he was referring to his son or to his son's Chinese lover. Nor was she disposed to find out. She wasn't seeking an argument but a receptive audience for her carefully conceived announcement. "There are three things I want you to know. Three things that you should know as family—just as Jeremy and Paul already do."

Father and daughter exchanged swift glances—but

again, not a verbal murmur.

"I am in the process of making a new will. You know very well, Hugh, that I'm not the kind of person who pays a lot of attention to that stuff. There are people in this very building who change their wills every month. Like Norma Beardsley, who believes that this form of blackmailing is the only way she can hold onto people's attention. I would like to be regarded as the precise opposite of that foolish woman. I am only changing mine because I've decided there are a couple of Foundations I previously had in mind that don't deserve a single cent and because my financial advisor (she deliberately suppressed Deborah's name) tells me that I have made a little extra on the market that neither of us was anticipating.

"That's number one. I'll go into details later when I've sorted out a few things." She meant when Rebecca was absent and she could do her best to persuade him to pay his religion-crazed daughter her allocation in small quantities and do his best to stop her foolishly handing it over to her coterie of money-grubbing Bible Thumpers.

"The second thing has already been touched on, but unfortunately it has to be emphasized. I am quite sure that something is carcinogenetically wrong down there." She pointed with her bony index finger to her body as she quickened her tone. "I want no fuss, I'll not have any drawn-out discussion. But I'd have you aware that it is my firm belief I shall not emulate the late Queen Mother and make a hundred. So just get used to the fact I could pop off anytime.

"The third thing comes right out of that—and it, too, I think you are now well aware of. I do not intend to be hospitalized for any reason. Not even for a single night!

Geraldine

What's that Spanish cliché that used to be on everyone's lips: *Que sera, sera?* Anyway, I've made up my mind, so the subject is closed. You can take it as an extension of my earlier decision to remain here and not go into some repository for the senile.

"So that's it. No discussion but I am now telling you officially that a) I have decided not to live forever, b) that you'll be getting a little bonanza, and c) that I propose making my final departure from this very apartment All of the above final!"

Geraldine clapped her hands in mock school-ma'am dismissal. Her son said nothing, merely bowed his head, but her granddaughter burst into tears.

Chapter Fifteen

The Greatest Plans

The phone lines hummed computer screens danced with words. Geraldine's pebble of declarations rippled to unexpected places. Her own old eyes blurred with fatigue and her lips grew leaden with overuse. And that was just from an anxious, overlong and unsubtle email from Jeremy who had heard from his father that his grandmother's inheritance was intended for all the family.

There was also a phone call from a Mrs. Haggar in #101 enquiring which day Geraldine was leaving Mayfair Apartments and how much she wanted for her place. She at once suspected that the Building Manager had been yakking—and so accused an innocent and surprised Deborah of gossiping with him. (What she didn't know was that before leaving the premises when she'd made her trinity of pronouncements, son Hugh, instead of following custom and leaving his own orders with the janitor, had instructed his daughter to tell Anton Molosovich to keep an even closer eye on her grandmother as she was contemplating a variety of rash enterprises.)

With prayerful admonishments and extortion of paternal promises, Rebecca, had done her father's bidding—even including his crafty hint that the Serb would financially benefit from what was tantamount to a spying job on his ancient occupant. When she left, adjusting an unseasonal hand-knit shawl and shuffling sandaled feet beneath an ankle-length drab dress, she held up her hand in what could easily have been mistaken as a blessing. In fact the Eastern Orthodox Molosovich was confirmed in his conviction that she was a witch or sorceress and was only persuaded to carry out her request by the suggestion of some money—which he rationalized he must accept, if only for the sake of his loquacious and still bossy parents who (he was secretly relieved) had remained in Kosovo.

An email appeared from the attendant in charge of raptors at the Greater Vancouver Zoo. Would she be interested in procuring (paying?) for a pair of American badgers (*Taxidea taxus*) from the Nicola Valley? Another from the same zoo source asking her to subsidize the purchase of a pregnant Grey Wolf (*Canis lupus*) from the Pink Mountain area north of Fort St. John.

More surprising—for Geraldine already suspected her grandson of being loose-tongued and probably of having by now alerted even the animals at the zoo of her generosity and potential bounty—was the ungrammatical and typo-littered email from her Jesus-besotted granddaughter. Though, mercifully for a sensitive atheistic like Geraldine, religious terminology was conspicuous only by its absence from Rebecca's rare missive.

"*Dearest Gran: You must have been very surprised at my silence when I did what Dad asked me and went with him to your lovely West End high-rise the other day. But I knew* he *was going because of what Dr. Caskie had told him of your condition and that he wanted me to hear anything you might say about what might be coming his way whenever you should pass over.*

"My Dad is what you might call a bit suspicious when it comes to money—Mum was no help in that respect as I expect you do know very well—and he is always worrying where it goes and whether anyone is robbing him. I tell him NO as did Jeremy when he was still around to help me out and wasn't just crying or yelling over his so-called friend, William.

I am doing my best to be honest Gran, and that means I must tell you that I am not mentioning any of those things regarding my faith which I know upset you, and over which I have to keep quiet as my Pastor says. Like Dad used to say all the time to Mum till she upped and left—you have to agree to differ—*which they never did and which is hard for me, Gran, being as I am, a True Believer.*

I was meaning to walk over to you when you said those things at the end in your beautiful apartment—about the money we are all going to get and not all of it going to Jeremy and that new friend of his. But I know you do not like fuss and have taught me to keep quiet about the deep love I have always had for you—especially when you wrote so nice that postcard from Montreal when Mum upped and left Dad, and again (I forget where you was) when we learned about Jeremy not being as other men.

Anyone at First Gospel Alliance will tell you how proud I am to have a grandmother who has done so much science to help the halt and the lame. They also know that whatever you thought to leave to your little granddaughter would go for her health and comfort in old age and not to our Hug the

Heathen Mission *or anything of that nature.*

What I am wondering is whether we should meet without Dad being there and we could discuss things on our own. I could take you out to lunch if you like. I saw a nice café just around the corner from where you live. Do you know it? Then I could discribe my life as it truly is and not perhaps as others have said it is, and perhaps I could discribe what truly good ways your generus bounty could go.

From your devoted granddaughter, Rebecca Woodbridge.

Geraldine was at times an irascible person but she was never an impetuous one. She may have had a short fuse where people were concerned but years of patient lab observation had given her a long one in dealing with the rest of life. Reading Rebecca's clumsy email—which she did three times—made her feel very cool. Indeed, ice cold. She saw it as somehow a further blot on her already unsatisfactory family.

One result of her granddaughter's missive was that Geraldine called Deborah to plan a council of war over all her greedy supplicants. However, instead of implementing an irate decision to eliminate all these beneficiaries from her will, her friend persuaded her to leave a significant sum to each family member, and to seriously consider (Geraldine was not yet entirely free of skepticism) a sizeable chunk to The Greater Vancouver Zoo rather than responding to individual requests from that quarter.

Then and there they drew up a document, which Debbie witnessed and duly promised to send to the Kerrisdale lawyers with whom Geraldine did business only by mail. (She loathed lawyers and refused on principle to sit down with one of them.)That item disposed of, the old lady suggested a mid-morning beverage before settling to further matters arising from the precious trinity of decisions she had announced to Hugh and Rebecca.

Debbie had plans of her own for later that morning but there was something about Geraldine's demeanor that made her suppress them. She mentally postponed her trip to the Lawn Bowling Club with Lilly Malleson followed by lunch and a substantial walk through Stanley park, to the Ferguson Point Teahouse, as was their Thursday custom. Debbie was soon relieved that she had. Before her Jameson's had reached her lips, Geraldine had launched into one of the elaborate statements that her friend knew from experience would ultimately conclude with a question demanding a careful answer. As usual they were sitting now on the balcony and Deborah took quick comfort from a distant Mt. Baker that looked like a giant ice cream cone, and at the nearby expanse of that was an almost Mediterranean blue and as calm as she could ever remember it.

"I have been taking your advice very seriously, you know, Debbie. There are times that I've been so good I wanted to vomit!" With which confession, Geraldine allowed herself a generous swig. "But of course, there are limits. For instance I'm not going to allow that miserable Molosovich in here to pry whenever my son puts him up to it. In any case, that way I'm doing good to both of them. I'm curbing the caretaker's curiosity on the one hand, and preventing Hugh from living in a dream world where I'm a complete imbecile on the other. As if I didn't know he blabs down there whenever he visits!"

Deborah was very still. Her friend's apparent awareness was rather too close to home. Hugh, after all, was very much prone to blab to her too…

Mercifully, Geraldine continued. "And I can deal with the nosey and would-be interfering rats in this building by just refusing commerce with them. But that leaves my quasi-literate granddaughter—she of the religious delusions. I should tell you that she came to visit with her father and that I received an ill-spelt email from her in consequence. I've already told you that I informed them I was considering augmenting their inheritances by a small degree. So perhaps it is not surprising that greed showed through every sentence. But I think there is more than just cupidity in her motives.

"She asked me out to lunch at that dreadful place around the corner and even worked hard at omitting the name of Jesus—which in speech, of course, she invokes with every bloody breath. Now, from your long experience of ill-educated girls, whether they have caught this religious malady or not, what do you think I should do? Something which would not let her fall into her father's error that I am gullible, but which would nevertheless assure her I have a reserve of goodwill for her—just as I have for her brother, even though it is harder to muster in her case."

She smiled across at her companion. "I know I am quite wicked in putting this kind of stuff on you, my dear. But you were such a help with Jeremy and Paul. You don't know Rebecca half as well, of course. But that could be an advantage. I'm sure the child's religious tattle would get on your nerves and her horizons hardly extend beyond the sentiments of a tabloid newspaper. But she is a woman of thirty or thereabouts—still of child-bearing age, anyway, and mentally incapable of serious intellectual purpose."

"Now you sound like the old Geraldine. 'Serious intellectual purpose' indeed!"

But her host wasn't about to give ground. "If to be your kind of saint means to flee common sense– then I'll remain evil if you don't mind!"

Deborah quickly softened. "I meant no such thing, my dear. You're far too old to surrender your mind, and I don't think you could be evil if you tried!"

Geraldine was mollified. As on the subject of Rebecca she wanted to be. When Debbie suggested she should agree to the restaurant invitation for starters, she concurred immediately. "I know the food is shit, but if I explain why to her it will not only contribute to her culinary education but perhaps make her realize how much I'm prepared to sacrifice for her. *Have* sacrificed. I've eaten down in White Rock when she and Hugh have prepared the meal. It is one of the reasons I've given the place such a wide berth. Not, mind, that I ever pretended to be a cook, Debbie. Never taught my son what I couldn't do myself. But I taught him as a child how to write out a cheque and started to take him to the better restaurants at an impressionable age. You know how I hate the presence of children with their jumping and screaming when I eat out."

Deborah couldn't remember the last time her friend had eaten out but didn't mention it. She knew the flood had crested and that Geraldine would soon return to a balanced conversation.

"Actually, instead of that hole next door I was going to suggest we go to the Sun Sui Wah in Richmond. She's probably never had *dim sum*—you know how parochial those Christian groups are—and the Sun Sui Wah is top-notch. My favourite!"

Deborah was human. She couldn't resist temptation. "I remember Paul taking you there and your saying afterwards, how much you enjoyed it." But she was still Geraldine's long-lasting, if wary, friend. She added no garnish.

She was rewarded with a quick look but no eruption. "Funny that you should mention young Paul Wong. I, too, was thinking of him. Now, Debbie, this is a long shot and you may think it too much so, but I recall Paul telling me he has a brother. Two of them in fact. Here come the "ifs." If I could arrange it so that Rebecca could meet one of them—both of them perhaps—and if something should spark between them. That is with only *one* of the Wongs, of course, then perhaps it could prove the very best thing that had happened to my granddaughter since her mother abandoned her for that rascal. Chinese food could only be an improvement for her. And my experience of Paul suggests that his genetic bank might well prove her salvation."

"And, how do you suggest all this come about, my dear. By a fairy wand or something? It's—it's not a role I see you easily playing…" she tailed off.

Geraldine leaned forward on her tubular lounge chair. "Precisely, darling! That's where you would come in. I could talk to Paul and see what he says. If he thinks neither of his siblings suitable, then I don't doubt there are dozens of cousins. He comes from quite an *enormous* family.

"We could meet whatever boy it turns out to be, right here—best with Paul I suppose—then we could all drive to Richmond to meet Rebecca. It would be a sort of halfway point for her and so neutral territory, if you see what I mean. Then you could have a chat with Paul and I could

scout out the lay of the land between the two young people. There would be no need for Rebecca to know any of
this beforehand. I would reassure her when I phone her
that her inheritance was assured. Might even be increased
a little, if the prospects suggested it."

Deborah mockingly shook her head. "Dr. Geraldine
Butterfield, I never thought I'd hear you advocating
arranged marriages—let alone playing the *matchmaker*!"

Her friend pretended to pout. But she too remained
in jesting mood. "Then I never thought of you, my dear, as
Cardinal Richelieu or Wolsey—the Royal Adviser. Then
what is history but The Great Recycler. The Chinese are
firm believers in that kind of thing, don't you know. When
that Paul is here interviewing me for his book, I find so
much to admire. To be so young and yet to so appreciate
his elders...." She paused judiciously. "Pity they went
through that stage of binding their women's feet in
thongs."

She, too, now looked out over the beckoning bay. "As
a matter of fact, Debbie, he's due here tomorrow for a very
important session covering a crucial point in my career. I
could drop him a hint then about finding a relative for
Rebecca. It might be the starting point of the girl's salvation—though I shouldn't be using her ridiculous language."

She turned faded blue eyes back from the sweep of
land and sea to the wrinkled and white-haired presence of
her closest friend. "But of course that all depends on your
agreeing to my plan, Debbie. On your approval and co-
operation. Otherwise the whole business is just a dead
duck."

Debbie nodded, toyed with the cold remains of her

coffee. "And the last thing we want around here are dead ducks," she agreed. "So certainly, Geraldine. Would you want me to be your chauffeur again or should Paul be allowed to drive us?"

Geraldine thought back to their last excursion. "I think it would be most fitting if Paul were to drive us to Richmond with whomever he has brought along. That would give us a moment to size the lad up—and make any last-minute arrangements that might occur to you."

Chapter Sixteen

All Kinds of Jeopardy

Geraldine couldn't wait. These days she always felt a biting at her heel. So she called Paul before he was due to visit her.

"I am looking forward to your arrival. I have important things to reveal for your tape recorder or whatnot."

"I am also looking forward to getting together again, Grandmama. I have good news about Jeremy and me."

"We are not talking artificial insemination and miracle births I hope?"

"Not quite. But we have found a lovely little apartment which is equidistant between the zoo and the city and thus perfect for both of us. We were going to ask your advice as to whether to rent or buy. Both are options for this place in Port Moody."

Geraldine had an immediate sense of where that "advice" would lead. She decided the moment couldn't be more opportune for her to put in her own request—one, moreover, that wouldn't cost anyone money—whereas she felt that wasn't likely to be the case in helping her "grandsons" secure a nest.

"Excellent, Paul. By the way, you mentioned your having brothers. I am wondering if one or the other was single and looking for a companion. My granddaughter, Jeremy's sister—and no, she isn't as bad as I'm sure he makes out—is in sore need of such. And from knowing you, my dear, I immediately thought a Wong would be right up her street."

His silence brought a peremptory: "Hello? Are you still there?"

Yes, Grandmama I'm still here. But you see, my brother Charles is married with a family in Nanaimo. My kid brother, Andy, well, shall I say he takes after me? He's looking for a Jeremy himself, that's what Andy's doing."

"Am I right in thinking you told me you also have cousins. On your father's side that is? More Wongs?"

This time, no pause. "There's my cousin Walter. He's 33, a lawyer, and single. His last date was Monica Cohen, the daughter of the hardware chain. But wait a minute! There's also Norbert. Norbert Wong is thirty-five and he already owns three pharmacy stores. Getwells? He's a bachelor also and goes to the United Church where he sings in the choir. Doesn't that sound promising?"

"That *Walter* sounds more interesting. If there's time, perhaps we could go into him a bit more when you're here. After I've given you all the details of that chapter in my life when I put my career in jeopardy—for the sake of a man, at that!"

But Paul was reluctant to let go of the thoughts she'd stirred in him. "Of course, Walter's frightfully busy. He's a very successful criminal lawyer. I'm not sure he could easily slip down to White Rock. I guess it would depend on his caseload."

Geraldine got down to business. "It wasn't White Rock I was thinking of—but Richmond. That excellent place you took me for *dim sum?* We can settle details when you are here, Paul, and not over the phone. But my idea was you would bring him here first so that he could meet both me and Deborah and then all four of us could drive to the Sun Sui Wah where we would meet Rebecca who at the moment is prepared to take any advice I might give. And now I can't wait for your arrival to hear about that charming little apartment you mentioned and which I'm already dying to see. Anyway, I shall expect you within the hour."

By the time he arrived, Geraldine had not only put out an anemic gin and tonic and a hefty Laphraoig for herself but a handful of frayed and slightly fading photographs of herself and a laughing man, both in white lab coats, of which she was going to allow him to select one for their book, and two or three letters from which she was prepared to read but none of which would be leaving her possession. When he was duly seated amid the sea of furniture in the L-shaped living room (less distracting than the balcony, she decided) she began with her measured lecturer's voice. But as this only appeared to keep his prominent black eyebrows permanently raised, she soon dropped to a more conversational tone. "We shall be talking today of deception. Of a man I knew, back in the 1950s when I was back East, who became a close friend as well as a colleague at Columbia. A man who became my friend, not in spite of but because he was an unmitigated liar."

Deception, liar, this *is* going to be interesting Grandmama. Was it an attraction of opposites?"

"If I knew precisely what it was, Paul, he would have

long ago been forgotten. Human alchemy is never simple. But don't interrupt. Let me get the sequences right and due illumination will most likely come."

Paul thought of the awesome apartment he and Jeremy had discovered and of the role Geraldine could play in their securing it. "Sorry, Grandmama. It's your show and you must call the shots." An internal bell buzzed, reminding him to preserve some elbow-room. "Unless I think you're skipping and I need the info to make the section work for the book."

He smiled, but she knew he wasn't kidding. "That's just being professional and you'll never get me to argue against that! Anyway, the man I'm talking about was named Malcolm Burfield and he was appointed Assistant Dean of Gynecology & Obstetrics about the same time I joined the Faculty. For several weeks I had little or nothing to do with him. The plain truth was I was pissed off that yet another man should be appointed to a position I personally felt should be held by a woman. Besides, he had almost movie-star good looks and several women on my staff made fools of themselves over him, pretending they were in love with him and wasting whole wads of our time discussing his private life. Or something he'd been overheard saying. Or even inventing things about his sex life.

"It got so bad that I was forced to let one of my juniors go. She appealed and of course, my male superiors over-ruled me. But I'm happy to say she had the decency to leave Columbia very soon after. I had to speak very seriously to another stupid girl, and—not for the first time—I had a flaming row with Dr. Rivers, an evil old biochemist who resented my appointment over him and who screamed at me in the library that if I had any guts I would

have volunteered for the post that Malcolm Burfield had
been given, regardless of the fact—as he bloody well
knew—it had nothing to do with my discipline.

"So when I finally did bump into Malcolm—it was in
the Staff cafeteria when he asked me if he could join me at
my table—there was already a whole pile of reasons why I
should have said no and kept my distance. Now, I don't
have to tell you that all the good looks in the world would-
n't have altered my opinion. But I do have to tell you that
before we had finished our lunch I was beginning to feel
sympathetic towards him."

She broke off to look up and smile at Paul—"I was
also thinking he was probably queer, what with those looks
and that easy way he had with everyone. In my book, lots
of minorities work harder to be agreeable just to earn
acceptance."

Paul resolutely remained silent. He wasn't about to
play spokesman for the gay community for his adopted
'Grandmama.'

"Turns out I was quite wrong. He had a wife—and
she had two or three predecessors. But that didn't emerge
until much later. All I learned then was that he hoped his
successor would be a woman and that, surprisingly, he
knew far more about my field than anyone I knew outside
it, except perhaps that young woman from Vienna, and my
work overlapped hers. But Malcolm's knowledge—indeed,
sympathy—for the work of others was not only outstand-
ing but suggested something more to me. I had the feeling
right there—and it has never left me—that this man was a
genius. And by that I don't just mean owning to an incred-
ible amount of knowledge—after, all, I was no ignoramus
myself. And as you already know, I have always striven to

keep my boundaries as open as possible and link the relevance of my work to that of others.

"I also shared with him the ability to make imaginative leaps in one's research. Plus we both shared an enthusiasm over the science of our time and the belief that we were on the brink of a series of medical discoveries more significant and informing than ever before in human history. The genetic factor was a special cause of excitement between us.

"I don't want to give the impression that all this took place over just one lunchtime. Our lunches together became commonplace and within no time we were dining out in Manhattan, attending the Metropolitan Opera together, and he had visited my Upper West Side apartment for drinks. I never visited his place though. Nor did we ever behave as other than good friends who were both scientists sharing similar visions. In fact, Paul, I can say that throughout my career I never felt closer to any colleague. I never had a closer friend with whom to share quite private thoughts. I hardly need add that I had plenty of colleagues convinced we were lovers and who went about gossiping that I was in cahoots with that other, shadier, side of him that was soon to become public knowledge."

Geraldine paused, sorting thoughts, perhaps editing them. "What happened was an utter surprise for me—though I doubt for him. I should add that Malcolm, over all those months—and it was a year before things began to really unravel—provided me with a complete account of his life to date. I learned that he was an only child of Australian parents, he certainly had an Aussie accent, that he was born in Perth and that his father had died when

Malcolm was six. He told me that he and his mother had moved to California when he was a teenager, and that he had attended high school in Pasadena and subsequently Stanford University, followed by grad work in medicine at UCLA. His stepfather was a marine biologist and his mother had become an executive with a film studio until her unfortunate death in an auto accident when driving in Baja California.

"He was now without living relatives, he observed, and insisted he had given none of his three wives any children. He was divorced from the last of them and was dating a girl, ten years his junior whom he'd met at The Church of the Resurrection on 53rd Street, which he attended somewhat irregularly.

"I never met her. Then I have no proof whatever that any of the stuff he provided me with was accurate. But I had no specific reason to doubt him until that day the Dean came to me and bluntly informed me that Malcolm was under investigation for false credentials, that the Administration had reason to believe that he was a total imposter with no medical qualifications whatsoever—and no university background they could verify. Nothing, in fact, except a suspected serving of time in San Quentin Prison for imposture and fraud.

"Well that's the outline, Paul. Now the *inner* reality. There was never a moment, right up to our last meeting in my office on campus when he said goodbye, grinned and shook hands before the police took him away, never a single moment that I regarded him as less than a friend. Nor cease to genuinely like him. But for months, of course, I had had growing reasons to doubt his veracity.

"Never anything flagrant. God! he was good at lying!

But not everything added up. Let's say they added up to fifty-nine when it should've been sixty. He never contradicted himself, like saying he did something in one place and later made it elsewhere. But there was just no way I could make the years fit with his all exploits. They were sometimes too few, sometimes too many. Then I began to realize that each "chapter" in his life ran like a movie script. They were all too smooth, too crammed with incident. There were no gaps, no forgetful moments for which he had to apologize. Did you know that someone's account could sound natural, consistent, plausible—all those things—and yet too pat at the same time? Well that was my Malcolm."

Paul thought he'd have burst had he not put his question: "And—and you said nothing to him? No questions?"

"No questions—because I knew he'd always come up with the answers. But it was more than all that. I didn't *want* to hear him argue his way out of things. What I wanted to know was *why*? Why had he chosen to create and live a life of fiction? I wasn't interested in such matters as where did the made-up elements end and reality begin. What ate at me was how a great and imaginative mind—and I never, ever doubted him those—could escape the thrall of fact and truth.

"I wanted to wear his moccasins" she added, using the expression Paul had first employed with her, "and understand, but it was then I realized I was just as much a prisoner of things as he was. Only diametrically opposite things—if that makes sense. I learned I was constitutionally, emotionally, incapable of escaping the claims of things observed—and accurately recorded. I was bound by the manacles of upbringing, genetic inheritance—whatever you like—to the prosaic. Whatever else my imagination did, it couldn't create; there was no room for fantasy in my capacious skull! But Malcolm—a crook, an imposter, in the world's eyes was nevertheless closer to a Beethoven or a Michelangelo than I could ever be.

"That was the reason I stood up for him at meeting after meeting. Even when they threatened my own career if I didn't furnish evidence of his dissembling. I wasn't about to discuss it with *them,* but even if his whole life proved to be no more than a tissue of lies, I knew there must be psychological motives. At any rate, I wasn't prepared to surrender my friendship for a bunch of pompous academics who really detested him for his brilliance and flair—yes, he *did* know his stuff!—and not because he was an incorrigible liar who loved to flirt with the danger of being found out.

"He was sentenced to ten years in a New York penitentiary for his latest escapade and the most ambitious of all his masquerades—all of which, incidentally, had a medical context. I never saw or heard from him after that. I think he knew at that last meeting that although we would never meet again, I bore him no ill will.

"What he didn't know, could never know, is how profoundly he helped me to see myself—however inadvertent that was and however screwed up his motives. He taught me, Paul, how circumscribed my kind are. And he also taught me the attraction of human opposites for one another. And it was by doing that he showed me the true gift of friendship. If it hadn't been for that phony gynecologist, that deranged fantasist and all his concocted dreams, I wouldn't have the likes of you, and Deborah to call my friends."

"Yin and Yang" said Paul' "I've never heard it put that way."

"*Yim* and yang' echoed Geraldine, slightly mis-hearing him.

He didn't correct her.

Chapter Seventeen

The Bells of Hell Go Ting-a-ling-a-ling

Geraldine wasn't feeling well. She was, in the idiom she used exclusively with Deborah, feeling *tummy rotten.* Nevertheless she had allowed herself to be persuaded—though insisting she be accompanied by her friend, Debbie, plus her grandson and his Paul—to attend the special Reception connected with the Engagement Announcement of her granddaughter and her fiancé, Paul's cousin, Walter Wong.

None of her circle had dared spell it out but Geraldine was well aware that this markedly premature festive occasion, usually preserved for marriage itself, had been prudently advanced (probably by Paul) in light of her age and the persistent rumors about her health.

This time Debbie drove, the two of them in pantsuits of differing shades of brown, with summer frills at cuffs and necks (in spite of its being September and the weather wearing a chill, grey frown), with Geraldine further distinguished by both her smart tan suede suit and her large, mannish wristwatch with a fresh Velcro strap around her ever-thinning wrist. They both sat up front in the elderly

Volvo, having arranged to meet the boys outside the venerable Foo Chow restaurant in Chinatown.

Jeremy and Paul were standing there in blazers and ties with Rebecca and Walter Wong in tow. The latter stood hand in hand, Geraldine noted with approval. Then so were Jeremy and Paul but she ignored that. This was Rebecca's and Walter's day, she rationalized, and it was towards them she walked stiffly with the aid of her cane—only inclining her snowy head at the boys and asking as an aside, whether they were enjoying their new apartment, as she passed. Debbie walked in her wake.

She broke custom as the group entered the restaurant in letting Walter, at his gentle insistence, take her arm instead of her friend. Rebecca was instead accompanied by her brother Jeremy, and Paul and Deborah took up the rear. It was all rather too formal for Geraldine's taste, but that was nothing compared to what they found inside.

Arranged in a huge horseshoe in the rather cramped space leading down two steps to the tables (which the restaurant had entirely rearranged, making them, too, into a horseshoe) was an assembly of Chinese in Sunday formality, ranging from the very elderly to excited small children, all patently expecting introductions to the little old lady, with her mixed race entourage in line behind her, and Walter. It turned out that every single person waiting to greet her was related to the latter and she wondered aloud whether the Lower Mainland at that moment was actually Wong-less.

Walter spoke in Chinese to a very old lady at the center of the horseshoe—Geraldine thought she might even be a coeval—and in response the bent figure in a bright blue pant suit, broke into convulsions of laughter and waved a very bejeweled hand in every direction including that of a portly Chinese gent in a dinner jacket whom Geraldine had thought was the proprietor of Foo Chow's. Walter explained that indeed he was, but that he was also a Wong and his own second cousin.

Before she had shaken hands with the last of the waiting Wongs—save, that is, the hordes of children who refused to stay put and scampered and yelled to a degree that reminded her of her own grandchildren in their horribly raucous and rambunctious youth, Geraldine was dying to sit down. That, however, was not only related to the state of her bones but the sight of a bottle of what looked happily like Ballantines, placed at the center of each and every table.

She wasn't mistaken. And once more Geraldine affirmed the wisdom and taste of the world's most populous people. A loud shriek made her think briefly of those little hooligans. She sighed, even while nodding firmly at Paul, who was now her neighbor, as he suggested pouring her a Scotch. If only Chinese children could acquire the delightful solemnity of their elders at an earlier age...

The seated assembly were arranged in quite different patterns from when all were standing. The principal guests, Rebecca and Walter, sat at the center of the curve while the rest of the guests took their places according to no discernible plan—save a tendency for the men, especially the younger ones, to sit separately from the women. The few Caucasians sat either at Geraldine's or the adjacent table. Hers, at her request, stood as close as possible to the entrance—for reasons she refused to specify.

If the excellent whisky—it proved on closer inspection not to be Ballantines but Johnny Walker Black

Label—was a magnet for her attention, a merciful slackening of internal pain (which she was convinced was profoundly abetted by her consumption of this alcoholic beverage) also contrived to keep her settled and in reasonably good spirits. She was able to turn to Paul for a more detailed account than he had hitherto supplied as to the progress of the presumably affianced couple and their reception from the family at large.

Paul was in good humor, too, particularly as Geraldine had generously furnished the down payment for his and Jeremy's new apartment, leaving them happily free of a mortgage. He told her that the welcome accorded Walter and his Rebecca could possibly be interpreted as communal relief that there were still hetero Wongs. On the other hand, he added, the presence of himself and Jeremy, along with his brother, Andy, who had turned up at the Reception with a handsome Cuban lad in tow, was also an encouraging sign of the times.

Jeremy then told his grandmother that he had been given a further fiscal raise at the zoo and been promised executive rank when he acquired his UBC credential. She was somewhat relieved to hear this—dismissing an image of her grandson as a Balkans Field Marshall— and even smiled across at her son, Hugh, who had arrived late and had been seated with his daughter and her fiancé at the larger center table. Family now attended to,Geraldine could afford to turn to Debbie seated on the other side of her, and comment to her that there was nothing like the choreography of potential breeding to bring disparate people together.

Then Geraldine's pleasure was ruptured by a horrible noise. It started as a faint but annoying chinking sound at a table close to the potential bride and groom's. In seconds it had grown to a sustained and deafening roar that assailed her hearing-aid and ravaged her pain-sharp nerves. Louder and louder it grew as more and more people were lifting spoons and banging them incessantly against glasses properly reserved for their whisky.

When she could stand it no longer she screamed at Debbie: "Why on earth are these people making that fiendish noise?" And as if she were a modern King Canute, the noise receded. Slowly at first and then, as the volume descended, distinct pings were heard and finally, the chink-chink-chink of the acoustically retarded or was it from a handful of obstinate hangers-on?

Even before the last chink of glass, Deborah Tregaskis was enquiring the significance from Paul who, looking askance at Grandmama's distraught appearance, replied to her rather than his interlocutor. "It is intended as a merry encouragement for the betrothed to kiss. The more they are reluctant to do so in public, the more their friends bang their glasses to persuade them. It is an old custom. I'm not even sure it's Chinese."

"I'm bloody sure it isn't from Luxembourg," snorted Geraldine. "It must be from some place where every bugger is deaf."

Debbie half rose from her chair to placate her elderly friend, but Geraldine had herself decided to shore up her irritation. She forced a smile on Jeremy, who was about to quake from her previous expression. "Isn't it amazing how sweet the sounds of nature are—at the zoo for instance—compared with what we humans get up to. I am so glad you have found your zoological niche, Jeremy, however precarious. And now your sister is about to find her socio-erotic one! I wonder what on earth we can find for your father. Perhaps something along simian lines. His first wife was rather hirsute. Perhaps next time he visits you at the zoo, my dear, you might—."

Whatever quality of spouse she had conjured up for her son, Hugh, the assembled company was never to know. For at that very moment the glass chinking broke out again. More spontaneous than before, and, if possible even louder. Geraldine was on her sensible leathered feet long before the din had crescendo'd, had successively yelled goodbye to the boys and waved to the other tables, and clutched Debbie's arm before declaring she must return home immediately.

In the car she confessed to her bewildered friend that other, nether parts of her anatomy, rather than just her ears, had really informed her abrupt departure. Debbie wasn't sure which explanation to believe. All the same, when they got back to the old lady's apartment, she hung about until she was able to see her friend safely in bed. When she called her goodnights, though, and let herself out, she was far from convinced that Geraldine would stay tucked up for very long...

Chapter Eighteen

Epilogue

Geraldine fought before calling Deborah. Fought with herself, that is. In fact there were two battles raging in her. One was in her body, where illness threatened to be the victor. The other was in her head, where she couldn't decide between the conflicting desires to be alone at this dark moment or seek the succor and support of others. As the pain grew she knew she needed her friend—if for no other reason, than to help her decide who else she wanted to see before all power of decision was taken from her.

Debbie was there almost at once, as if she had been hungrily awaiting such a summons—which perhaps she had. She was soon knee-high once more in a jumble of furniture supporting the several rejected canes, of black wood or aluminum foisted on Geraldine by wellwishers, or heirlooms of brief hospital visits for a hip transplant and a knee operation, that she latterly conceptualized on her decreasing outdoor walks more in terms of assault than support.

These malignant souvenirs were joined by a couple of

spurned walkers that had also been consigned to the heap of unused and unwelcome insignia of old age and its concomitant indignities. More favored but now equally part of the bric-a-brac were the further piles of miscellaneous objects acquired over a life lived on two continents and three countries: icons of nostalgic reverence, of pride and eager talking points, rather than irritation and shame...

Debbie had hardly navigated all that discarded history before she sensed something major had befallen her perversely indomitable friend. It wasn't just the lack of being offered the ubiquitous scotch, or the perky welcome that Geraldine usually supplied. The mood of the room was altered; subdued, darkened by the distinct modification that its owner's spirit had undergone. Debbie immediately caught the lowered voice, the ever more bent figure—details confirmed when the old lady, instead of briskly preceding her over the small window step out onto the balcony actually paused, turned and held out an unsteady hand. "Help me out, will you Debbie. Bit rocky today. That's why I asked you up."

Debbie was there, supporting her arm before all that was out. It was then, their bony bodies close, perhaps a new, sweetish if faint smell emanating from Geraldine coming to Debbie's nostrils, that she knew an irrevocable notch of change had occurred, that more had happened to her companion than the rumpled passage of a night's sleep and a fresh back-up of decisions or questions from that restless and rebellious brain.

When Deborah proceeded to aid her friend onto her customary outdoor lounge chair, her offer was refused. "Help me over to the balcony, will you, dear. I prefer to stay standing up."

Deborah also noted the gentleness of address that now displaced her friend's normally brusque commands. As she stood behind her and shared the view, she thought how small and frail was the figure in its blue-and-white check-housecoat, as the nonagenarian stood erect, hair blowing everywhere, supporting herself by placing out-stretched arm bones along the low balustrade.

A large white cruise ship, modernistic in its ungainly superstructure, was heading out the sunwashed bay. "Alaska is its destination I suppose," said Deborah. "With lots of fascinating places in between. There's Sitka and Ketchikan that friends tell me are worth the cruise for themselves alone."

Geraldine didn't answer. At least not that particular topic. "I'm not going to St. Paul's again, Debbie," she suddenly said. "Whatever happens, I'm *not* going there—not even for a check up. So to hell with their arrangements!"

Her friend had heard all this before. Many times. "Don't upset yourself, Geraldine. Everyone knows that. Goodness knows, you've made that plain enough."

A longer pause. "I've heard from Hugh this morning. Then old Caskie. He was obviously put up to calling me by my son. It's quite obvious that our leaving that Chinese wedding party so early has upset all of them."

"You really can't blame them, can you Geraldine. They're all concerned for your health—and your leaving the way you did quite understandably startled them." She didn't tell her friend that both Hugh and Jeremy had called her, too.

"Paul telephoned as well. But that was different. He told me that now our interviews were over he'd have something to show me before the end of the month. He was quite excited. Said it was going to be a terrific book." She now did turn around. Sufficiently for Debbie to see her expression. She was smiling wanly. "Pity I didn't feel up to responding in kind."

She looked so drawn, so exhausted. Debbie's compassion welled. "Why don't we go inside, Honey. I'm sure you'd feel better sitting down."

Geraldine underwent transformation. Those blue eyes frosted, her back went ramrod and color flooded back to her voice. "I intend to stand and I want to be out here. And while I've got the will—"

(Debbie secretly substituted "willpower")

"I will do just that. I love this balcony. Are you aware, Deborah, that we are perched over the second busiest port in North America? After New York? And certainly the most beautiful urban bay. In a hospital bed you could be in any old place. Just like those great American hotel chains— you can't tell which continent you are on, let alone country you're in. The same crummy pictures, the same phony furniture…"

Deborah was saved a longer speech by the sudden advent of a glaucous-winged gull to the right of Geraldine's gnarled hand, which was still hovering about the balcony for support. It wasn't exactly surprising as Debbie knew she made a practice of feeding them there. But it was propitious, nevertheless. "Look at those expressive eyes!" she said quickly. "And have you ever seen such white against the gray? I think he's been using a box of Tide, Geraldine."

"If Debbie's strained humor was lost on her friend, the presence of the large and so pristine-looking bird was not. And when it began to clap its yellow beak and successively raise pink legs, the old lady was entranced. "*Larus glaucescens*," she announced, "and by the look of the plumage, all the immaturity has gone so it must be at least four years old. Will you go into the kitchen, Debbie, and fetch the remains of my breakfast. On the plate on the table. Hardly remains," she added, "as I couldn't eat anything."

Deborah did as she was bid, pleased to see the change in mood and only hoping the gull would stay and entertain Geraldine in her brief absence.

But when she got back to the balcony she dropped the plate of buttered bread which shattered and scattered at her feet. Before her, Geraldine lay in a crumpled heap, the bird flown. She was at her friend's side in an instant, gently lifting the featherweight body to its feet. She had rocked with instant relief in seeing the old woman was conscious, and now, as she grabbed her more tightly and led her, not towards the chaise longue but towards an upright chair, was happy to hear her muttering, even though it was to herself.

"I'm not leaving...staying...my home...ambulance he wants... won't get me in it. I—I..." The babble gave way to gurgle and died away altogether as Debbie got to her to the chair and sat her down in it.

The gull returned precisely to the same spot on the balcony wall; eyed the bits of bread about the balcony floor. Geraldine forced her head up. "Why don't you feed it," she instructed.. "Can't you see like all gulls it's always hungry?"

Debbie picked up two portions of bread that had fragmented on impact, took them over and laid them on the balustrade where Geraldine had been standing. The perverse gull immediately hopped down to the deck to pick up the other slice it had spied. Debby peeked over the balcony, why, she wasn't quite sure. Perhaps because Geraldine had. Right there below, at the high-rise entrance, was a white vehicle. It took a few seconds of its continual light flashing for her to realize it was an ambulance.

She turned at once back in the direction of the chair where she had left a huddled Geraldine. The gull hopped out of her way but refused to open its wings preparatory to flight. Before Debbie reached the chair she was filled with premonition. Huddled had turned to slumped. The small-featured face uplifted to the sky, blue eyes inquisitive as a ferret's, halo of white hair—all now utterly still, all now responding to a different *maestro* from that she had served seconds earlier.

Before she bent her own silver-white head forward for confirmation, Debbie knew what she would find. She thought of the ambulance and a whole lot else, and wanted to both laugh and cry.